Church of the Oak

Sheila R. Lamb

Triple Fire Press

Contents

"...Patrick then requested our saint to make with her own hands that shroud, in which his body should be wrapped ...in that shroud then promised him by St. Brigid..."

Life of St. Brigid, John O'Hanlon

CHAPTER 1

Brigid

I stood, unable to move, to breathe. Maithghean found me. His eyes locked with mine. My first thought was to run back to Patrick. My second though was they will find him. Protect him.

Where was the Brigid who could turn to stone? In my moments of hesitation, Maithghean and Elían rushed to me, took me by each arm, then pushed a bitter paste into my mouth with a drug Elían hid in the folds of her pocket. Not the Test drug...something else. A datura concoction, I guessed.

Dathi argued for me as they dragged me toward the waiting cart, that I was one of their line. "Her training here is incomplete. We were just ready to-"

"She belongs at home with her father," said Maithghean. "She must finish her training in Fotharit. Her home."

Dathi tried. He reached for me as they pushed me into the wagon. Elían's drug was already taking hold. Dathi signaled to the warriors at the gates but Raven lay her hand on his arm. She shook her head slightly at the warriors. "She's not ours, Dathi."

"We agreed to train her, Raven. To accept her into our order."

"You agreed. And we haven't accepted her yet. We can't afford a battle with all of Leinster. As great as her talent may be, she's not ours."

Before I sank into unconsciousness, I saw Raven signal the warriors again. They surrounded Dathi, three men with swords around the old druid. "Make sure Dathi stays in the fort," said Raven.

Then Raven spoke to Maithghean. "We will keep our peace with Leinster."

And so I was returned. The potion Elían made stuck in my throat until it dissolved. My mind and body were heavy, too heavy to move. I could hear but I couldn't speak, couldn't move my limbs. I heard Raven's betrayal.

I wish I had blended into the stone. The ancient power was within me. I'd done it once before on the battlefield years ago. But they had been with me then, the Danann. They were not with me now.

After days of traveling in the wagon, I was brought to my father's house. Elían fed me the drug daily. Forced water down my throat. Gave me bread which I ignored. I slept.

When I awoke, I had a sickening fear I'd be left with Maithghean, a lifetime as his slave. For whatever reason, I was in my old home. Perhaps Father stood up for me, for once. But Maithghean was there every day, prodding, questioning. I refused to speak. I didn't talk to him, not to my father, not to Elían. They even brought in my old friend Lomman. I didn't speak to him either, but our eyes met. He knew. He would help. Of course I would escape again. But the escape needed to be permanent.

I needed the strength of a king and an army of warriors behind me.

CHAPTER 2

Patrick

Light broke through the haze and touched Patrick gently. Disoriented, he reached for balance on the branch of the oak tree in which he slept. Hunger gnawed at him. If only he could get his bearings, a sense of direction, he would be home. Home. With his father and his mother. Years had gone by. What if ...? He refused to think in that direction.

He'd found a harbor and sailors who said they would take him to Britannia. For a price. He was forced to row through European rivers and spend agonizing winters in Germani land before they returned him to the Sabrina River. Now, he was home—or close to it.

Peering through the branches of broad green leaves of oak, he found he was alone. No warriors to hide from, no dogs to give chase, no sailors to give commands. He made his way down the wide trunk, embracing the thickness and using rough knots as handholds. In the early summer morning, a rustle of leaves signaled their goodbye.

Finally on solid ground, British ground, he took in his surroundings. I must be close. Frustrated, he looked around the thick oak forest and the trickling stream at his feet. He should know this land, every curve of it. The incomplete memories nagged at him.

"Dear Lord. Please help me. I'm so close to Bannaven Taberniae. Please." He drank his fill of water from the stream and continued toward home.

Patrick stumbled into the village, almost by mistake. People glanced at him oddly; he was certain they thought him a beggar, searching for scraps. He was dressed in rags. Scraps of his wool tunic, the blanket made by Brig - no. He would not think of her.

Bannaven Taberniae had changed. There were more houses than when he left. When he was taken. He wound his way through the maze of thatched homes that should have led to his family's villa. He turned the corner to find it wasn't there. A few pieces of stonework, remains of a fountain centered in what was now a marketplace.

The last time he'd seen his family's house, it had been engulfed by flames. It was gone. He panicked and turned in a circle at the spot where his house should have been and bumped into a vegetable stall, earning an angry rebuke from the owner when a bin of carrots cascaded to the ground. Where are they? My parents? Brawen? A broken cry escaped his lips and, as if from a distance, he heard the wild animal sound of his voice.

"Please," he croaked, and then realized he had spoken in Irish. His mind worked, searching for his native tongue. He reached out to people, strangers, drawing angry glares.

"Calpornius?" He questioned the next passer-by. "The tax collector? Do you know him?"

"Patrick?" A man's voice startled him from his despair.

Patrick tried to reply, but his tongue stumbled over the long unused accent. "Linus?" Linus, his best friend during soldiers training, his friend who had been at his house the night of the raid.

Linus grabbed him in a huge bear hug, lifting Patrick's feet from the ground.

"My God, man! You're alive! This is incredible! Brawen said you and the others were still alive."

"Brawen?"

"She's fine. Fell in love with one of the Silure sailors that rescued her. They're living on the coast. House, children...pagan as can be, though." Linus made a face. "Your father doesn't look too kindly on her."

"Where is he? Where are my parents?" He freed himself from his friend's embrace, choking on the Latin. "Are they...?"

Linus held Patrick at arm's length and studied him critically. Linus was obviously wealthy, a clean white toga showed his status. Almost clean. Patrick's dirty rags had left a streak of dirt. His eyes widened, and Patrick was certain he was ready to tell him a horrible truth. Instead, Linus pointed to a road to the south. "They built a new home along the road to Aquae Sulis. Your parents are fine."

The heavy weight of fear lifted from his chest. He smiled at his old friend, incredibly happy to know that his family still existed. Linus pulled him by the hand.

"Come on, Patrick. I'll lend you my horse. We'll ride to your new home together."

Patrick awoke and stared at the white walls of his comfortable room and listened, confused...Eamon? Conall? It was only the sound of his father in the next room, turning in his bed, murmuring in his sleep...Patrick lay his head back on his pillow...I'm home.

An unknown servant had opened the door when they arrived at the new house, sprawling with fountains in the front, ready to send him away when Linus spoke in his defense. His mother came running, her robes flying behind her. She stopped short at the sight of him until Linus said gently, it's him. He's been enslaved. She reached for Patrick. Come, we will get you in a bath and send for your father.

She sent a servant to him, a young man with sharp features that reflected the geography of Gaul. The slave bathed him, cut his hair, shaved his beard, and stayed silent.

Patrick wanted to say something, to say he understood, to say he was sorry that his parents kept slaves too, but he couldn't. Exhaustion overtook him yet even as he leaned into his father's shoulder, he saw the face of the Gaul who had bathed him.

Patrick was home for a full moon before agreeing to meet Linus at the tavern on the Aquae Sulis Road. Linus insisted on plying him with ale, determined to hear all the details of his years away. Patrick had not spoken of his experience to anyone, even his parents, who waited for his story with patient solicitude. He'd told them in broad strokes about the kidnapping and being forced to be a shepherd, but that was it. He mentioned no names, not Milliuc, not Maura, nor Conall, and certainly not the druids.

But, after a few hours, the ale loosened his tongue and he felt like a carefree boy again, out late at night with his best friend. So, he bragged. He bragged about the woman he met in Éire, a beautiful druidess, once a goddess.

Linus chuckled. "She must have been one of a kind for a servant girl, hiking up all that way to find you. Maybe you were one of a kind then? Did all the maids show up in the middle of the night and distract you from the sheep?"

Patrick choked on the drink he had gulped down with enthusiasm.

"No, Linus," he grinned as his friend slapped him on the back. "She had been a goddess. Then a magical druid. Not a servant girl. A real goddess."

Linus rolled his eyes and Patrick banged his mug on the table, insisting on another refill.

"Right, my friend. A goddess. Surely you dreamt the whole thing." He laughed again.

Patrick turned to him with an intense clench of his jaw. "She was real."

The words were whispered, deadly serious. Tension filled the space between them. Patrick looked away first. Linus was right. Maybe he had imagined the entire thing. Too many years alone on the hillsides, so he invented Brigid in his final months of loneliness.

Linus stretched his arms overhead and then reached for a few coins in his pocket. "Come now, Patrick. My wife is waiting for me, and your parents are waiting for you. Calpornius will have my head if he knew I joined in the inebriation of the next decuriones. Somebody's got to collect the taxes, and tomorrow it will *not* be you. You will be nursing a hangover."

Patrick stumbled out of the tavern after Linus, only to stop and vomit into the hedges.

Now, alone in his room, he regretted his actions. Why had he told Linus about Brigid? Why mention her at all? Linus probably thought he was insane, or incredibly drunk.

The next decuriones closed his eyes, but the room spun around him. He opened them, trying to focus on a single object, anything to stop the intoxicated dizziness. A gold cross hung on his wall, and he stared at it as the room stilled.

Decuriones. Linus had mentioned that it was expected for Patrick to follow his father. Did he really plan to become a tax collector? In the weeks since his return, Patrick saw that the Empire was in trouble. Gone, in fact. Britannia was in a state of perilous flux. For whom would he be collecting taxes?

He turned over in his bed, slowly, as not to disrupt his churning stomach. The room spun again, and Patrick focused on the cross.

God. Prayer. These things made sense to him. They were his only comfort during his final years in Éire and on the terrible journey through Germania. He finally made it home by the grace of God and no other. He wished for the comfort now that often came to him in church.

"Dear God," he began his prayer again. He didn't have anything specific to pray for, to ask for. The one thing he'd wished for, for years, he had. He was home. For a while, he had asked for Brigid's appearance, that she would come to Brittania as they planned...but God didn't answer those requests. Still, he prayed for some sign of her. A message. He prayed but he knew she would not fit surrounded by the cool, frescoed walls of his parents' home. This would not be her place, even if she did step off of one of the trading ships at the port. And what was his place?

He was home but it didn't feel like home. Not just the new house. He no longer fit his parent's idea of a son. He was an adult now but hopelessly lost. He was supposed to begin training in the tax code, the thought of which made him wish he were tending sheep. Nothing fit but prayer. God. God who led him out of the wilds of Eire. Patrick gladly accompanied Calpornius to each Mass; his father was proud that his once wayward teenager now knelt in thanksgiving before a priest. One day soon, he would have to follow his father into the tax office, pick up the scroll and leather bag, and never set it down.

Prayer somehow connected him still with Éire. Patrick couldn't explain it, but there it was. The strong pull. He resisted. Pushed it away. Languished instead in the peacefulness of the quiet church. It wasn't the words of the priest he heard, but the tone, soothing, as if he could lull himself away into a dream. It had all been a dream, what happened over the sea. That other place. Milliuc, Dathi, the farm. Brigid.

Here, he could recite the liturgy. Listen to the soothing Latin. Escape from the memories of cold, of loneliness. What he wanted was to stay forever in this peaceful room and talk quietly to God. Patrick closed his eyes and allowed a new vision for his future to form.

CHAPTER 3

Patrick

"I'm applying for the priesthood." Patrick nervously waited for his father's reaction. Even as an adult, he felt like a boy around his father.

Calpornius lifted his eyes from the scrolls that scattered his desk.

"Son, I've arranged for you to begin your mathematical training in Britannia next month. I wish Dyfed were still here, but he passed when you were...gone. You'll need to review your figures before taking over my position here."

Patrick shifted from one foot to the other. "Father." His voice wavered and he took a deep breath. "Father, I will begin seminary school in Gaul in the spring. Brother Albunus has it all arranged." His father shifted scrolls from one side of his desk to the other. "He'll escort me to the seminary in Gaul. It's one of the best, and after my studies I could be placed anywhere. Even Rome itself."

"Your grandfather was a priest, Patrick. It's a difficult life. Your wife and children are forced to move from parish to parish at the whim of the church. It's no way for a family to be raised." Calpornius filled a satchel with the scrolls, tax statements to be delivered to the citizens of his town. How was it any different from that of a soldier? Patrick thought, but knew his father spoke from his own experience. His grandfather had moved his family several times throughout Britannia, making Calpornius more adamant to settle in Britannia.

An image of Brigid flashed through his mind, and Patrick recalled a memory - no, a fantasy - of their house and farm in Éire. Fantasy. Dreams of a lonely shepherd boy. Their one night together was perhaps a more realistic dream than most. Memories of a life before, and a man named Padraic, was all imagination.

Only the call of the church comforted him, silenced the constant movement of his mind in the tranquil hours spent in prayer.

Patrick placed his hand on his father's arm as he stood to leave. He didn't want him to leave the room with the conversation unfinished. "I will leave for Gaul after Easter to study at the seminary." *Please, Father. Please understand my choice.* Choice. How long had it been since he'd made a choice of his own? "Let me leave with your blessing." He hadn't wanted to beg before the man he admired—and missed—for years. Calpornius adjusted the heft of the satchel over his shoulder. He glanced at his son, a look that Patrick couldn't decipher. The decuriones left his office without reply.

CHAPTER 4

Brigid

I stayed in my father's house. A new house, rebuilt since my anger caused the old farmhouse to burn. I was his servant. His prisoner. But at least not Maithghean's. I considered escaping to Mother's community but it was too dangerous. The Fotharit druids would use her against me and Mother deserved peace in her new home. Let her believe I was in the west, studying with Dathi.

West. Where Patrick waited for my return. Alone. I promised to be back after three days. I was filled with guilt. Longing. I had to let him know what happened.

I was confined to Fotharit and banned from all druid ceremonies and meetings. "You're not a druid," Father repeated to me each time he left for the oak grove, leaving me at home. "You are your mother's daughter. A servant."

When I refused to speak to him, Father offered me an escape, one he'd tried before. "You know you have options, Brigid. You can marry Tagdh. He's a high-ranking bard. If you married him, maybe he would speak for you. Ask the druids that your training continue."

I said nothing in response. *Maybe* Tagdh would speak for me. Maybe, and more likely, Tagdh would follow Maithghean's orders and keep me in servitude. And I couldn't imagine marrying someone who wasn't Patrick.

I milked the cows. Fed slops to the pigs. Sold eggs at the market. Cleaned my father's house. I was followed by guards when I went to the stable, when I went to the fort, and when I went to the granary.

Maithghean visited Father's house. He too let me know there was a way out of my imprisonment. "Another Test of the Ancients. Now that you know your past." He didn't know the extent of my memories and what was left to be discovered. "If you share your knowledge with us, with your tribe, we can revisit your druid training."

I turned away from him. I took the slop bucket to the pigs. The pig sty was one place Maithghean would not follow. I wondered why he didn't force me into the Test as he'd done before. Why didn't the druids drug me and take me to the oak grove? Fear, I realized after several days of puzzlement. They had discovered something before, anger of the Ancients, to give them pause not to do it again. At least not without my acquiescence.

Bacene especially enjoyed watching my downfall as guards followed me on my daily chores. He'd smirk as he'd pass by with his bard's bodhran. Sena did the same at the granary. I spoke to no one. I milked the cows. Fed slops to the pigs. Sold eggs at the market. Cleaned my father's house.

I watched from a distance as messengers came and went to Dunlang's chieftain lodge. They were given proper guest lodging and shared news between tribes. They let Dunlang know of a new ship with supplies or slaves at the harbor. When a feast was shared with a visitor, I was not invited. I stayed in my father's house with two guards at the door. When I was alone, I thought of Patrick and the summer we shared in the pasture. Our memories slowly revealed themselves, life after life. The night where we were together as we should be.

When I could no longer stand reliving my days with Patrick, I reviewed Dathi's plan, our plan again. Making me some kind of arch druid because I had passed the Test wouldn't work. Too many others would question the claim or stew in common jealousy. I didn't want that kind of title anyway. There had to be a way to renew our beliefs, to bring the Ancients back to the people. Druids should be trained in the ancient path. Not like this, where Bacene watched his sister, his acolyte counterpart, endure imprisonment for refusing a life-threatening test. The key was to get novice druids and druids-in-training away from their tribes, to avoid the in-fighting and politics. We had to return to the beginning.

As another wheel of the seasons passed, my only reprieve was to herd our flock of sheep. The grove closest to the fort allowed the guards to watch as I led the sheep back to the farm, along the forest's edge. No wagon or mules for me. I wasn't allowed to have anything that might help me escape. That's where Lomman found me. He hid behind thick oak trunks, out of sight of the warriors.

"How can I help you Brigid?"

I nearly jumped out of my skin until I saw it was my friend. "Lomman!"

"What they are doing to you is terrible. You're a gifted druid and they are evil. Jealous. Let me help you."

I paused and glanced behind me. The guards were sitting, leaning against the fencepost, playing knucklebones. I heard the toss and rattle of the sheep hocks. Of course they were bored watching a woman do chores all day long.

"Well, we can't set my father's house on fire. I already tried that." We smiled together.

"And," he added. "They won't believe me if I take a wagon to look for a lost cow."

"Did Dunlang find out?" I'd been caught up in my own misfortune that I never found out if Lomman was caught for helping me escape.

"He suspected. Maithghean definitely suspected. They couldn't prove it and I did return home with a missing cow. But I doubt they would fall for it again."

Dunlang. Lomman worked for the chief druid and I needed a messenger. He followed me along the forest edge as I led the flock toward home

"Please, Lomman, if you can...I need to send word to the western tribes."

He peered around a tree trunk. "I can try. There are messengers that come to Dunlang."

"I know. I've seen them in the fort. But only someone that you trust. Dunlang and Maithghean must not find out." I ran down the hill to round up an errant ewe. The guards were still leaning against the fort wall, totally oblivious to my leaving the pasture and going to the farm.

"What message do you need to send?" Lomman asked when I returned.

I took a deep breath. "Please, tell no one but the messenger, Lomman. Do you promise?"

"Of course. You're my friend. You're the only one who has helped my family."

"I'm looking for a man named Patrick. I knew him in the west. He studied with the same druid I did. He might still be there in Foclut Forest. The druid to contact is Dathi. Only Dathi."

"I'll try." Lomman backed away into the forest.

Months passed. Cold rain. Ice. Flurries of snow. The months of gray clouds reflected my mood for another season. While in the market, I traded wool for eggs with Una, Lomman's mother. Through this, we devised a plan for Lomman to contact me, leaving simple ogham messages on fallen trees or boulders in the sheep's pasture. It wasn't safe for Lomman to try to get to my farm or to be seen with me in the market, since he was already suspected of trying to help me escape before. I waited hopefully to hear from him and he would let me know what the messenger said. But the winter cold left messages to wait until spring.

I continued my silence with Father. I supposed he thought he was helping me, by saving me from Maithghean, at least. It would seem difficult not to talk to someone in the same house for one year, then two, then three. I kept myself in a meditative trance while in the house. With a bit of magic taught to me by Raven, I could create a wall between Father and I. Block him off. That wall of energy also protected me while I slept. It took a good portion of my strength but I was able to ground again in the stables or in the pasture. Suddenly I understood why Mother spent so much time with the animals.

Father tried, now and then, to talk to me about the same things. Marriage to Tagdh. Sharing what I knew about the Ancients. Yet he refused to discuss druid issues. He never spoke to me about the changes in the Samhain ceremony or the winter Solstice. Blessings, Maithghean had asked in our tuath ceremony. Blessings to the warriors for the spring raids. Bring back more cows, more slaves. The gods were happy because we continued to win. I wanted to cry because I missed the father of my youth, the one who taught me about weather patterns and the power within a stone. He was gone. Or maybe he never existed.

Finally, the light broke at Imbolc. I was busy with the flock of sheep. The ewes began the lambing season and I spent much of my time in the stable. I checked on the birthing ewes. I used my druid training to make a poultice to prevent infections in the ewes and the lambs. Then I reached on the stable shelf for my blade and whetstone, to cut umbilical cords. Two stones fell from the shelf, the whetstone and another new stone. And that's when I saw the simple message scratched in with a few lines and slashes. *He's gone.*

Patrick. I breathed a sigh of relief before the tears came. Of course he was gone. I'd shown him how to escape, which paths to take, which roads to follow. For the thousandth time, I wondered what he thought, how he felt, when I didn't return. Guilt pierced through me. Would he think I left him on purpose? Did Dathi tell him what really happened?

I worked with the ewes as they birthed their new lambs. I remembered the time Patrick and I went through lambing a flock together. No. *Padraic.* That's how the memories came and I had to differentiate between the pasts.

I spent the weeks of late winter in the lambing shed. Gone. Patrick was gone. It wasn't supposed to be like this. Dathi and I were on the right path, leading Patrick slowly along. It was Raven who undercut us, who capitulated to Maithghean. I wondered what power he had over her or if a simple bribe was enough.

Britannia. That was it. I'd ask Lomman to find another messenger and send him to the harbor! I scratched lines on the other side of the stone and left it behind the large oak at the forest edge. And at the market, I handed Una sacks of grain and gold pins stolen from the druid stores as payment for her family and for the next messengers. They were to find sailors that traded with the Britons.

By the end of summer, three different messengers had no information. No one named Patrick had returned to Britannia. He should have been home by now. If he were hurt, killed, I would have *known.*

For another full circle of the wheel, season to season, I carried out a servant's duties. I didn't touch a druid torc or a healer's potion. I milked the cows. I fed the pigs. I sold eggs at the market. I cleaned my father's house. I learned to meditate in a trance while working. I reviewed ceremonies in my head, in silence. I connected with the Danann in my dreams.

I ignored Father's offers to marry Tagdh, I ignored Maithghean's offers of the Test with stony silence. We stayed deadlocked.

As the next Lughnasad drew near, my blood began to stir. Anger rose to the surface, my motivation. I sent for another messenger. Not for Patrick. For myself.

CHAPTER 5

Patrick

*L*iam and Nial chased after him as he started up the mist-covered mountain. "Holy boy, walk with us!" they called, laughing, trying to keep up with Patrick's long strides.

"No, I'm going home," he replied, and continued the steep climb upwards. A message waited for him at the summit. He must reach it before the mists broke.

"Holy boy! Walk with us! Holy boy!" They chanted as he receded into the mists.

The climb was difficult. He struggled uphill, with labored breathing. He knew the message would be there, he knew where to find it. His feet sank into the damp peat, the rich smell of soil he knew so well. Julia, the ewe, walked next to him and nosed him along, as if he was a newborn lamb.

His hands reached out and grasped the angular corners of the quartzite boulder. Power surged from the star shaped stone, lodged into the mountainside. It hummed beneath his touch.

"Here," he said. He sat beside the quartz, waiting for the mists to clear. The clouds parted and he saw all of Éire before him, a green jewel in the center of the ocean's blue. There was the lonely hill, where he spent years as a shepherd. Farther off, he saw a small speck, which he knew to be Milliuc's house. Beyond that, his bird eye view took him to the opposite coast, where he knew Lupida and Darceca waited for rescue. A sharp, stabbing sadness overwhelmed him, and he reached, hands outstretched, to his old friends across the land.

The letter landed on his palm. Balancing the parchment, he leaned against the star stone, calmly, knowing this would decide his fate. It opened with a whisper...he smelled damp air after a rain, fresh milk, and clover.

"Join me, Patrick," she said. "Return and we will be victorious."

Patrick awoke in his dormitory bed, startled. Looking from side to side, he tried to identify the voice of his dream. He slept in a room with a dozen young men, eager for the priesthood. No female entered here.

He pressed his cheek against the plaster of the wall, grateful for the coolness. Summer in Gaul was hot, humid. It was Brigid. It had to be. He squeezed his eyes shut in the pre-morning dawn. I've dedicated my life to God. I will live, as did the Apostles, in Holy Communion, teaching the words of Christ. Why now? Why return to the island that enslaved him? It must be the pressure of his final studies or the unknown future. He didn't know his parish assignment. His mother begged him to return to Britannia, but he was prepared to go anywhere ...Britannia, Parissi, even holy Rome itself.

Dawn rose and the student priests awakened with the light. Patrick decided it was a dream that startled him awake. A dream, nothing more. Yet the scent of clover stayed with him.

He bent his head in prayer and knelt against the pew with his fellow seminarians. Silent meditation offered peace. Fear had gnawed at him and his fellow students for weeks. Could they assume the duties of a priest successfully? Could they bring converts to the Church during these trying times? Invasions weakened the empire. Poor leadership nearly broke the back of anything related to Rome. Rome, as it had been, was gone. The Church must intervene. Patrick secretly questioned if he could serve communion without spilling the wine.

Calm yourself. Allow the Lord to speak through you. His mind quieted.

Patrick! Return to Éire!

He jumped up at the sound of the voice, causing several heads to turn in his direction.

Éire needs you!

Standing, he scanned the chapel, trying to find the source. It's not God. It's her. It is a woman's voice speaking to me... He scrambled for alternatives. The Virgin Mary. That must be it...Mary, Mother of God, holy of holies... He knelt again, composed. He would speak to the Mother of Christ.

"We turn to you for protection, Holy Mother of God.

Listen to our prayers and help us in our needs...."

Patrick, Éire is your destiny...

Claudius elbowed him in the ribs. "Patrick, control yourself. One hour of silence, then we receive our assignments."

"I'm sorry, Claudius. It's just –"

"Shh...Father Germanus will hear you!" Claudius edged himself away, determined not to be associated with Patrick's outbursts.

Patrick gripped the wooden edge of the pew beneath him. He closed his eyes again. Please Lord, please Mary, Mother of God. "Save us from every danger, glorious and blessed Virgin..." Banish the voices from my head...Her voice...she —who left me alone.

He saw the copper hair, the green eyes, felt her smooth skin... he remembered before: Padraic, the land of flax and sheep and peaceful family after years of struggle... the scent of clover... He tasted her sweetness as he did that summer, her breath warm on his shoulder...

It's me, Patrick. Please return to Éire. We need you...

Do you need me? Because if you needed me, you would have come before now.

Angelus bells rang, breaking the connection. He lifted his aching head and watched the next seminary student follow Bishop Germanus into the rectory. The bishop spoke to each priest individually to inform him of his parish assignment.

Patrick fidgeted. The men around him filled the room with whispers. They were too keyed up for prayerful silence once the first of them had been called away.

Patrick wondered where his placement would be. He could go anywhere once controlled by Rome, which meant almost anywhere in the world. Except for Éire. Ireland. The place of his captivity. The one island not ever under Roman rule. If any group of people needed the Lord's light, it was there. A land bound to slavery. A people bound to druids. He recalled the first Samhain ceremony he witnessed and the sacrificial piglet. He still cringed with revulsion. They needed God's light, these clean white walls. They needed to know Christ, not the darkness of autumn's ghosts.

How could he even consider going there? Why should he go back at all? Certainly there were plenty of pagan communities in the world. He wondered, achingly, if Lupida and Darceca survived. Were they still alive? He hoped they found good men to protect them, as Conall did for Maura...even if it was too late for freedom. He thought of Maura, Liam...he hadn't thought about their welfare in years. Liam would be grown now, possibly with children of his own. Was he still at Milliuc's farm? His children would be free...the third generation was granted full citizenship into the clan.

Patrick closed his eyes and images of the farm returned. They worked hard each day...he remembered the harvests in the fields, backbreaking work...his isolation on the hillside, tending to the vulnerable sheep...only the pagan festivals a reprieve from labor...and his only chance for human contact...Milliuc himself. The thought of him used to cause disgust in Patrick, but now it didn't. Patrick sat in the chapel surrounded by nervous whispers and pondered Milliuc's angry red face with his drooping mustache. Now, he didn't hate him, nor did he fear him. He pitied him. He wished the burly warlord could know the peace that he knew at long last. Patrick could show Christ's love, cleansing, calming, soothing.

Dathi's face floated before him...he shivered in the summer heat. Patrick realized he didn't really hate the old man. Instead, he feared him. He feared the way the druid's eyes pierced his soul and discovered his secrets. Yet it was only now he considered it. Did Dathi have something to do with Brigid's disappearance? She'd gone to Dathi to gain her druid status. What if she hadn't left him at all? What if she were manipulated in some way? Or worse? He'd blamed her for all this time, never considering another fearful option. He had to return. Odd, he thought. I'm at peace thinking about Éire, about slavery, Milliuc, Dathi the druid. Patrick reveled in the moment, astounded at the tranquility that washed over him, even as his classmates were tense with nerves and expectations. He contemplated the miraculous transformation that permeated him in a matter of minutes.

He could wait no longer. He ran to the rectory, pushing new priests aside. "Father Germanus!" He called frantically. "I'm going to Éire. To Ireland. I will start a mission there!" Patrick said, running into Father Germanus's office, breathless, feeling like a young boy, giddy with delight.

"Patrick, have you lost your mind?" Father Germanus looked at him as though he had. "You will go where the Church sends you! Go outside and wait your turn!"

"No, Father. I will return to the island. That is where I will go. I have been called."

"I don't allow it. The Church does not allow it. No formal mission exists, not since Palladius."

"Then I will start one. I will continue where Palladius left off. There are pagans there that need leadership and who must see the light of God. I must go. The people need me."

"Patrick, you can't go! You are not sanctioned by the church!"

"I know the land, I know the people. Father, please."

"Patrick, this is unlike you. You're acting like...like..." The older priest stumbled for words. "Like a teenage boy."

"I know, Father. I'm sorry, but –"

Father Germanus shut his door, making the next priest-to-be wait in line a little longer.

"Your homilies are superb, Patrick. I know of no other priest who shares the passion as you do. You will have no trouble finding an audience."

Patrick clenched his hands together, waiting expectantly for permission from his superior.

"Is there a woman involved?"

Patrick paused, unsure of how to answer.

Father Germanus continued. "Several young men here have wives waiting for them at home. Have you a wife in Éire?"

"No."

The older man squinted at Patrick and rubbed his hand across his chin. "You will go whether I allow it or not, won't you?"

"I believe I will, Father. The calling is strong, and there is a need for a new mission there." Patrick stood a full head above his mentor.

"You have my blessing, and only mine," said Germanus. "It's up to you to secure your appointment from the Vatican."

CHAPTER 6

Patrick

Patrick struggled with his Latin script. Writing letters to Britannia was a chore. He scratched the words with berry ink on vellum. His house grew dark. It sat at the back end of the monastery, so each morning he could look out at Armagh and all he'd created: the beehive quarters for the dozens of monks, the tall cross of the chapel that quartered each sunrise.

He hadn't lit candles, and he'd told his monks, who usually did those chores, to leave him alone. They did as he requested, especially when they knew letter writing was involved. He strained his eyes as he searched for errors. If he misspelled a word, he'd begin the entire letter over again on a costly sheet of vellum.

The bishops in Britannia expected annual reports on the Christian conversion of Éire. Since he had left without formal permission from the Church, he believed they were especially hard on him. Because of his impulsiveness, they were stricter on him, demanded additional updates, things not required from other priests. He'd never obtained the agreements from bishops and cardinals, an official requirement that Father Germanus encouraged him to complete. He'd left France, said a hasty farewell to his parents in Britannia, and sailed for Éire. She had called for him. She was there.

When he arrived at Lambay he stood waiting, as if Brigid would greet him. He'd hired a man with a wagon to take him to the nearest tuath. Taking advantage of his host's hospitality, he gathered supplies, food, and water. He'd hoped, too, he'd find Lupida and Darceca. Maybe they were servants in a nearby village. He began traveling along the coast, keeping a wooden cross hanging by a leather thong prominently displayed on his chest. He visited tribes, explained about God and

Jesus. Told the people how he was freed from slavery. How he escaped, made it home, and returned again. God's will. His dreams were what gave him hope. His dreams were where Brigid appeared.

"They don't understand. They have no idea of life in Éire." He tossed the quill to the floor, but left the vellum alone. Patrick struggled to explain to the Roman church hierarchy how each section of land in Éire had its own chieftain. Numerous chieftains, petty kings he explained, dotted the countryside and owed loyalty to no one else. They didn't have control over their subjects' personal beliefs. Dunlang of Fotharit, for example, didn't demand his people accept Christianity and seemed to care less when Patrick preached outside the large ring fort.

It took time to visit all the minor and major chieftains. He had to explain Jesus Christ on their terms, in ways they would understand. Sometimes, they weren't very friendly about it at all. He'd met with resistance the farther west he traveled. He'd been kicked out of villages. Warriors roughed him up. Druids stared at him with cold, soulless eyes. One druid, in the far reaches of Connacht, threatened him with sacrifice. Patrick had taken to traveling with two guards from Fotharit for his safety. Odd, he mused. *I spent years trying to escape Irish guards, and now I ask for their protection.*

I will apply to be bishop.. He gritted his teeth at the harbored resentment of that thought, then corrected his bitter feelings. *No, I left without waiting for consecration, a process that would have taken years of my own free will. I must prove myself to the church. I must prove my worthiness. I must show them I can convert the pagans of this land.*

Why must I show them? His hopefulness gave way to rebellion, as he rubbed an ink stain from his oak desk. *Why should I care what they think? Why should the British bishops have any control of Éire? I'm creating something new, something different. No one in the church administration has set foot on Irish shores.* Those priests who joined him were friends from seminary, like Bishop Mel. Many of the monks who followed him were native converts.

Éire needed an independent church suited to its needs. The island had never been controlled by Rome. No need for its newly formed church to be in a Roman, via Britannia, model. No need at all.

Keeping an Irish church free of British control bordered on clerical treason. He wasn't ready yet...soon, but not yet. He wanted to try one last time. He'd return to Britannia in the spring and ask again for a bishop's appointment. He'd earned it. They should grant him the title. Even if he never had permission. Even if he flouted their rules. He'd earned it by hard work, not to mention life-threatening situations. He picked up the quill from the floor.

He closed his eyes and saw her, the copper-haired goddess who haunted his dreams, with a flash of green eyes and scent of fresh clover from the fields. Yet, she wasn't a goddess. Brigid was real, living in this land somewhere.

He'd practically run to Fotharit just over a year ago. Or had it been two? He knew she was there. He'd felt it in his bones.

"She's gone. Up into the forests. She'll stay there for a few days, then return," Dubhtach said when he asked the whereabouts of the tuath's young healer. A sore ankle, Patrick lied. Instead, he was taken to an old woman, Elían, who proclaimed his ankle looked fine and to keep it wrapped tightly in a cloth if it hurt. "Why did you ask to see Brigid?" she asked.

"Some people to the north said she could treat injuries. They didn't have anyone there."

"The forest communities," said Elían. "They barely make it. We've offered them shelter here, but they refuse."

"They said Brigid brought them food and medicine." He kept his perfectly fine ankle propped on the stool.

Elían looked him over. "You're curious about my apprentice?"

Heat ran to his face. "I'd heard her name is all."

"Patrick." She leaned over him, and he felt uncomfortable under the druid's close gaze. Her long gray hair framed her snub-nosed face. It was stupid of him to come see the healer alone. He hated to be alone with druids.

"There's a connection between you." A hint of a smile played on Elían's mouth. She stayed over him, hovered close. He wanted to get away.

What did that mean? He didn't know. A connection. A connection without explanation, without reason. "What did she tell you?" Anger rose within him. Brigid had exposed their secret to this heathen druid. He'd told Linus, once, drunkenly, in Britannia, but that was different. It was another land. Linus didn't believe him. These people, they believed. They believed in goddesses and fairies and the Danann. "What did she say?"

"You tell me," she whispered. "What is your connection to her? How do you know her?"

"I don't know what you're talking about." He pushed the old woman aside, forgetting that he was supposed to be hurt. "There's no connection. None at all."

"None?" Elían pulled her hood over her head. Patrick saw only her eyes peer from the hooded shadow.

"Go on, go to the feast. Pretend your ankle is sore and ask Maithghean about Brigid. Our chief druid might be able to tell you where she is."

When he was seated beside Maithghean at the chieftain's feast, he knew immediately why Brigid had run away years ago. The man repelled him. His hair and beard were long and unkempt. Maithghean reminded him of the raiders who spent days on the open sea. There was something sour, sick in his depths. Patrick didn't trust him.

"Elían told me you were looking for Brigid. She left this morning. She goes up to the forest a few days at a time. Why do you need to find her?"

Patrick gave the same story he'd told the old woman. What he didn't tell Maithghean was that Brigid wasn't in the forest villages. He'd passed through there before sunrise. He would have seen her. The bearded druid had lied to him. He realized this and the beard. That was odd. Most druids were clean shaven. Why was this one allowed to keep his beard?

Patrick understood they were hiding something about Brigid and that she was not there. He felt a catch in his solar plexus. Suddenly, he was tired, drained. "I need to sleep," he said. "I've had a long day of travel. Tomorrow, I'll tell you and your people about my beliefs."

Patrick spoke quietly to servants about the love of Christ. He'd met them the next morning as they wove cloth, milked cows, or herded sheep to pasture. When he showed them his ability to herd the sheep into a pen, the shepherds grinned and listened even more closely to his message. One-on-one was his first step in teaching about the new faith. He'd visit several more villages along the coast until he ended at Erc's community. Then he'd pass Fotharit again and draw in the crowds. This method gave them a few weeks to discuss the new visitor, his claims of slavery, his belief in a new god. Let them talk about how a slave gained his freedom. Ponder the idea of leaving. Of going south. Or north, to Patrick's land. As long as they knew it was God who granted their freedom.

Patrick broke fast with the druids. He was supposed to be entertained by a young man, Bacene, who poked fun at monks but Patrick failed to find the humor. He ignored the boy and eavesdropped on the two druids at the next table.

"This Patrick is the one we need to worry about," said Maithghean. "He definitely has...power. We'll invite him to a ceremony tonight."

"A ceremony?" asked Dubhtach.

"There are things he's not telling us. Elían has an idea of what they are."

"Elían?"

"Apparently, she thinks there is a connection to Brigid. I think our guest here might know more than he thinks."

"He's not druid trained, at all. He's not even from this land. How could Brigid have any connection to him?"

"Elían has made the potion. The herbs have aged since Brigid's test. They'll be more potent. The Ancients will know if there is a connection between them." Dubhtach left Maithghean on the bench, either angry or bored. Patrick's mind raced. Potion? Herbs? Would the Ancients help him? That's all Dathi and Brigid talked about, the Ancients. Patrick, for one, was tired of hearing about them. He wasn't going to risk his life in some kind of weird ancient ceremony.

He found the servants he'd spoken with and bid them farewell. He found the chief of the tribe at his house. Two men stood before him and a woman and young man, mother and son he suspected, were seated in the far back corner of the lodge. Patrick tried to see if they were free to move or if their hands were bound.

"You're always welcome here," Dunlang said and waved Patrick aside. He was red in the face and apparently had been chastising two warriors who stared at the ground. "Here, priest. You said you needed protection as you traveled? Take these two with you. They are useless to me."

"What about the two in the back?" He nodded toward the mother and son.

"Mind your business," said Dunlang gruffly. "Take the two you were offered."

Patrick looked back at the guards, young men, barely with beards. "Do they *want* to go with me?"

Dunlang handed him a fistful of knucklebones. "They'll follow that game anywhere."

Patrick's head ached now as he thought of his visit to Fotharit. How close he had been to Brigid but not close enough. He stared at the scrolls and letters on his desk. He closed his eyes and tried to comprehend the complexity of her. Where did she go? Elían and Maithghean made it seem she was living at her home as a healer. The guards, who now enjoyed a relatively easy life on guard at his chapel, told him a servant named Brigid had walked away. He didn't even know what that meant. A servant? Had they captured her? Walked away where? Perhaps the woman has all been your imagination run riot.

He opened his eyes and picked up his quill once again. Pushed her image from his mind. Pushed the glimmer of past memory farther away. God had a fine sense of humor.

CHAPTER 7

Brigid

Rushing water along the banks of the river greeted me. The solitary oak stood on the horizon, a faint outline in the fog. I recalled the battle held on the plains and the memories that revealed themselves. Power radiated from the sturdy trunk, and magic wafted from the leaves. They rustled in the stillness, urging me forward. I crossed the river at a sandbar and scrambled uphill, resting against the tree's roots.

The last messenger I sent for did not go west or to the harbor. I searched for a druid and a tribe who would support my plan. In my years in servitude, I'd solidified Dathi's original idea. The people did need to be taught about the Tuatha dé Danann but traveling from tribe to tribe was too dangerous and it smacked of vanity. So I asked who would be willing to listen to my ideas for a center of learning. And as I sheared the last sheep, I simply walked away from the two guards playing knucklebones at the front of the stable. I ducked under the pig fencing and walked into the forest. I took a circular route to where my blue cloak lay waiting along with a supply of dried venison, fishing twine, and a water bag under the oak tree where Lomman and I had met.

Warriors at the nearby fort's entrance sent word to Ailenn telling them I'd arrived. Dun Ailenn was a tribe who showed the most interest in the druid school. Ean, their chief druid, closely ranked Maithghean. The chieftain of Dun Ailenn, the tuath that carried his family's name, greeted me.

"We are honored to have the daughter of Dubhthach here with us." He welcomed me. Ailenn was a broad, tall man, with a full beard that seemed to increase his smile rather than hide it.

"Thank you, Ailenn." He'd greeted me as Dubhthach's daughter. He didn't seem to know that I was now a servant, not a druid-in-training.

"Fine, then. We'll meet over our meal and discuss it then." With a hearty slap on my back, the jovial chieftain escorted me to the guest quarters. He ordered his wives to draw water from the well and light the fire. I warmed by the hearth and let the women fill my mug with cider. The colors of their skirts showed they were women of high rank and enjoyed the business of company.

Ean came to meet me after Ailenn's wives finished bustling about. Unlike Maithghean, Ean wore a druid tonsure and was clean-shaven. Cutting his hair above his forehead allowed knowledge into his mind, a custom Maithghean ignored. Ean wore a long cloak made of a white spotted bull's hide, a luxurious show of his rank. He glanced at my blue traveling cloak and his eyes burned into me, searching for the truth. The messenger had told him to expect Dubhtach's daughter but it was clear I had no bronze or gold to show any sort of rank.

"You're young for such a long journey alone."

"I've traveled farther. I spent a season with Dathi, in the west."

Ean nodded in acknowledgment but hid any surprise he might have had. It was the plan Dathi and I had made that I wanted to propose. I needed the help of a strong tribe and a strong druid. After I presented the idea, then I would tell Ailenn and Ean the details of the Test of the Ancients and my current servant status. If they did not agree, I would leave immediately. Father and Maithghean would be searching for me.

I was seated near the head of the table, next to Ailenn and across from Ean. The rest of the druid order was seated down the length of the table. Platters of food were brought to us: bread, a mix of butter-soaked greens, clover, mustard, and trays of roasted venison and dried salmon. Servants filled our earthenware mugs with ale.

"I come from a tribe where we have great success at cattle raids and battles," I began.

"I know," said Ailenn. "Dunlang took half my herd a decade ago." Ailenn sucked on the marrow of deer bone, picked off the pile of remains on his wooden plate.

"But something is missing. Particularly among the druids. This is what I'm here to discuss." Both Ailenn and Ean raised their eyes to look at me. "Our druids are called in to counsel the chieftain in matters of battle, to read portends for the outcome, to bless the warriors and their weapons. What happened to the gods and goddesses who gave us this land?"

"Nothing happened to our gods," said Ean. "They have been and will always be."

"Is this true?" I felt the ancient Brigid stir within me. "How many children recall the Ancient Ones, without being told they are some sort of haunting spirits? Or fairies? How many druids connect with the Ancient Ones, really connect?"

Ean looked uncomfortable while Ailenn seemed to be trying to understand what I was saying.

I continued. "The Brehons uphold the Law, to be sure, but the rules are focused on prisoners of war and slavery, which is another problem. My own mother joined the Palladians in the north to be free of her slave status. They follow the Roman belief, the Christians."

"Truth be told, Brigid, we don't always give the Danann their due. Lugh at summer solstice and harvest time, Brigid at Imbolc," Ean smiled at the reference to my name, "but the minor gods rarely play parts in our rituals. As far as our servants and the Christians, I haven't heard enough about them to be worried."

"Brigid, did you come here to discuss current events? Why did you, alone, seek us out?" asked Ailenn.

"I would like to propose an idea. Dathi and I discussed this in my time there but now it is time to solidify the plan. If we had a school where druid acolytes could focus on their studies without being distracted by the politics of their tribes."

Ailenn shifted in his seat. I'd offended him. I didn't mean to, but I had to speak the truth. "Yes, full druids do go out to the battlefield. We are here to honor the earth as well as the cycle of life and death. We speak to the trees, the rivers, all of those elements of nature that the Danann represent, don't we?" I asked.

Ean nodded slightly to Ailenn. He agreed with me. His gesture gave me the courage to continue.

"Druids need to be immersed in our studies and focus on our connection with the land. It's the only thing that sustains us, and that is where the druids are losing strength. We go through rote rituals without really understanding why. We accompany warriors on raid after raid." I stopped. I couldn't risk having Ailenn against me. I wanted to use his land, a field closest to the sacred oak, to build the school. I could almost read Ailenn's mind as he looked at his spacious round house, walls burdened with shields and weapons, thick furs and blankets piled high along the walls, a table laden with food. He wasn't a weak man, and his tribe, outwardly, showed strength.

"Our people are divided." I pitched my voice and directed my comments to the entire table. All the druids needed to hear this. "We live insulated in our own tribes, except when we fight for cattle. Class divisions separate us: brehons, druids, warriors, slaves. First degree wives square off against seventh degree wives. All of this causes discord, rifts that can't be repaired."

A new voice spoke up. "Brigid's right. Kidnapping men and women from other tribes and forcing them to stay here won't work."

"Brigid, meet my daughter, Darlughdacha," said Ailenn dryly. "Call her Dar for short. She's a novice druid as well, on the seer's path. We thought we'd include 'lugh' in her name to bring in the sunlight, but unfortunately, she prefers the moon."

A few years older than myself, I guessed. She had long black hair and a pale complexion, like the color of moonlight. She smiled, a full, wide mouth like her father's. The kidnapping and slave issues rankled her, and came between her and her father. Ailenn stiffened his back when she spoke.

"What if we created a school where druids and acolytes from different tribes could share ideas, stories, medicines, rituals," I explained. "That would add to full druid training, which students could complete at their homes, if they choose. We could bring our people together again. This is what I am proposing and this is where I need your help."

Ean might be tempted to help me, if only to gain superiority over Maithghean. Neither he nor Ailenn seemed convinced at the end of our meal.

"Maithghean warned me you had some fanciful thoughts," Ean said mildly.

I set down my ale and faced Ean. "You shouldn't believe everything Maithghean tells you." My sharp tone betrayed my emotions, my panic. When had Maithghean contacted him? How did Maithghean know where I was? I took a deep breath in an effort to connect with the earth and reach for calming energy. This had to succeed. It had to. I wouldn't be able to return to Fotharit. I couldn't live in the Christian community with my mother. I risked everything for this plan to work.

Ean picked up his ale and shifted into a conversational mode. "Speaking of acolytes, aren't you still one? Why would anyone send their students to someone not fully trained?" This was the question I anticipated.

"I'm the daughter of Dubhthach. You know my heritage and my skills. I studied for a season in the west, with Dathi, where we devised the plan for this school. I've surpassed the third rank of healer in less than a year and have performed rituals since I was a child. As you may have heard, Maithghean took me from the west and I was brought home." I still refused to say I was a servant. A slave. Still, Ean was unmoved. "I've passed the Test of the Ancients." Ean blinked. Other druids at the table gasped. "So whether I'm fully trained...well, you'll need to decide whether that matters or not."

"How did you survive the test?" asked Dar. Her translucent blue eyes bore into me.

"I don't know." Her eyes captivated me. Blue, but not like Patrick's, whose sharpness pierced down to my soul. Dar's were cool, like poured milk. I sensed soul ties with Ailenn's daughter. We had known each other before.

"Why did they test you at all?" Ean asked. "It's dangerous, especially to risk a talented acolyte such as yourself. Death is the usual outcome. No one here has performed that test in generations."

"I don't know," I repeated. I couldn't tell him any more, not yet. Not until I knew Ailenn's tribe would protect me from Fotharit. My acknowledgement of the Test and Ean's anger caused an uneasy tension among the druids of Dun Ailenn. They began to argue amongst themselves about the purpose of the test and if it could be done safely. Some wanted me to speak more about it, but I refused. There were secrets I would tell no one.

"Come." Dar stood next to me with an outstretched hand. "Come with me." She led me out of the rancorous hall to a grove of oaks at the outer reaches of the fort.

"Listen," she said. A stream trickled nearby. A faint breeze blew through the leaves of the trees. The moonlight dimmed under a hazy cover of clouds. She touched an oak and the ground beneath it, illuminating the line of energy that ran between them.

I joined hands with her and together we felt the thrum of the earth's power.

Energy connected between us, back and forth, heat from my hands to hers, down her body, and into the earth. It coursed back through me, through the soles of my feet and through my hands, back into hers. A cycle, continuous. It had been years since I had shared druid power and I drank it in, like water.

"We will build your school," said Darlughdacha. "We will not let our people forget."

CHAPTER 8

Brigid

It was Dar who convinced her father. The school, she told him, would be under Brigid's vision. "It's her plan and we have the resources to back it."

"What does this get me?" Ailenn asked. "I'll lose the southern corner of my land."

"Think of the influence you'll have." She knew how to appeal to her father's desire for power. He was a king, after all.

Ean brought up the delicate nature of my situation. "Brigid, you are bonded to your father. You are his servant as was your mother."

My face burned. Even after all of these years, after knowing Patrick as I did, the thought of servitude shamed me.

"Yet," Ean continued, "you are druid-trained and you survived the Test of the Ancients. Survival doesn't happen unless there is intervention from the gods." I nodded, recalling a similar conversation with Dathi. "I've never liked Maithghean," said Ean. "But I also don't want to start a battle between us. Ailenn will say you are here under his protection, and the school will be guarded as part of Dun Ailenn. However, I will not train you on the druid path. Is that clear?"

I faltered. I was hoping that I could somehow, one day, earn full druid status. Until that happened, I was still considered a slave,

"You don't need the training, Brigid, and you know it," said Ean. "You've gone beyond what any of us can teach you."

"But -"

"It is only a loan that I will consider," Ailenn interjected, meting out his terms. "The man who used to farm the land you will use is old and tired and has no children left to work it for him. The plains by the river are used for grazing and an occasional battle. You don't have the cows to pay me what it is worth, but in time, if the school is a success, you will. You will have to pay me back."

It would take many cows to pay for that piece of land, and the school would have to be successful for many years to pay that price. I clenched my hands in my lap. What if it doesn't work? How would I ever repay Ailenn?

"The Test of the Ancients may have given you special...gifts...but you are not trained, and neither is Dar. Therefore, neither of you can teach acolytes beyond the second year. Two years maximum and they must return to their druid order. Beyond that, we'd have a revolt on our hands," added Ean.

Dar looked at me and she saw my disappointment. "One step at a time," she whispered.

"It takes foresight, Brigid, to see what you have. Our future is bleak. We will fall apart if something new isn't done." Dar believed wholeheartedly in the ideas I'd presented.

"Thank you for speaking to your father for me," I continued. "Now we just need to work out the details."

"Many of us can teach. I can train in seer-work, you in the healing arts." She told me of other druids and druids-in-training who could teach novices. "And we will remind them that the Tuatha dé Danann must be part of every lesson. This is our focus. Not tribal battles or winning chieftains."

Dar changed the conversation as we walked. "Tell me about the western lands and Dathi. You created this idea with him and their druids, didn't you?"

Patrick, I thought. "Just Dathi. His druids are as skeptical as ours here."

"Yet you've continued with this idea. Why didn't you stay in the west?"

I told her what happened with the Test of the Ancients, my escape, and my forced return. "Dathi took me in. As horrible as the Test was, it has opened...id eas...that I didn't have before. Dathi saw this and we wanted to share what I had learned. He didn't want to take it from me, like Maithghean..." I paused. I had no way of knowing Dathi's intentions, really.

"Is there anything else? I feel like there's something...well, perhaps I don't know you well enough to ask for more details. This is the danger of being a seer."

I smiled in agreement. Having a friend who could inuit your thoughts and emotions meant there would be little to hide. "Patrick. He was part of this, with Dathi and I..." How could I explain? Lover, friend. But it ran deeper than that. Lifetimes, back to the Danann. And now he had disappeared into the world. "He's gone now."

After our plans had been drafted, we walked with Ean and the Dun Aileen druids to the site. Ean wanted to bless the earth where we would build. We joined hands in a circle while Ean led the invocation. He asked for Danu's blessing on the land. "We call on the Old Ones, the spirits of the Dagda of the Rain, of Macha of the Wind and War, of Eiru of the Clouds. Lugh of the Sun. Banba of the Rivers. Fodla of the Earth. Brigid of the Imbolc light." Dar held my hand on one side and Ean on the other. As he spoke each name, energy coursed through me like an electric charge. They grasped my hands tighter and that charge spread through the circle. The Danann pulsated in the earth beneath my feet, restless, wanting, impatient. Send us your strength, send us your power, we will rise again, we will claim this land again. We were linked by the druid circle, by the roots of the sacred oak and by Danann beneath us.

CHAPTER 9

Brigid

A ilenn's tuath helped build roundhouses and larger halls and lodges, white-washed with lime. Dar's belief in the school never wavered. I was grateful to have a friend and supporter to help with the overwhelming tasks Dar and I planned together. The halls would be used for classes and a lodge for guests and meals. By spring's end, we completed round houses and the hall, complete with a courtyard to share hospitality with visitors. While they built, Dar traveled to find druid acolytes that would join us.It was too dangerous for me to travel. Not yet. Some chief druids questioned our ability and refused to send their youngest druids in training. But most, like Ean, supported the plan. If it wasn't outright support, they were willing to try. Everyone was tired of the fighting.

Ailenn's tribe donated a milk cow to us, and several ewes and a ram. The school's first year would be one of survival, but Ailenn's support guaranteed we wouldn't fail outright. By midsummer, students arrived. Over a dozen druid novices. All girls. I wondered why young men hadn't been sent. "They won't send the boys to an experimental school," Ean explained. "Too many young men are lost in battle, warriors and druids. They'll take a chance on the young women who will return in two years. If you fail, the home druids will have time to repair the damage."

Most of the girls were on the healer's path. A handful of others were seers, storytellers or musicians. "It's because you have the reputation as a healer," said Ean. "And Dar's as a seer. That's why they are sent here. Besides, do you really want to teach the sacrifice rituals?" He had a point. We all had to learn how to cut an animal painlessly. We had to learn the proper ritual for bloodletting. We had to learn to read the entrails. Most importantly, we needed to know when sacrifice was necessary. It was a powerful tool, not to be taken lightly. Sacrifice training would be taught at the home túaths.

I took a step back and realized that I changed Dathi's dream into my own, shaped it into something new. I wondered if Patrick would be convinced of it. The longer I was away from Patrick, the more I recalled his cynicism of druids. He'd only half-heartedly worked to remember his past, our past, and loved me for whatever reasons. He was never fully convinced of the Ancients, the existence of them. Still, with Ailenn's help I sent two more messengers, one to the west, and another with a ship of Silurian traders. Silence from Dathi. And no one knew of a man in Britannia named Patrick.

Alone one summer night, I sat in the courtyard for a silent meditation. Dar went to visit her father. A handful of guards at the gate protected me. Determined to learn what the Test of the Ancients unlocked for me, and Patrick, I reached down into the earth and called to the Ancient Ones. *Help me find Patrick.* I was surprised to hear their response. *Find your own powers first.*

I hadn't had a physical, sensory response from the ancient gods since that day on the battlefield, long ago. Find my own powers. The Test had unlocked knowledge of who I had been and who I was, but I hadn't truly accessed what I could. I had healing knowledge. There was plant and healing lore that I didn't need to be taught. I just knew it. Yet I had allowed myself to be taken from Patrick. I couldn't fight against Maithghean.

Remember, Brigid. Remember your life here with us, the Danann powers Brigid possessed. What is at the center of quartz? What happens when you strike it against flint?

I knew this. I'd studied quartzite since I was a child. Understanding washed over me. *Spark.*

Spark. Fire. It is at the center of your being. Stone surrounds you on the outside, and fire lights you from within.

I reset my concentration, reached beneath the surface of the earth and of myself. Drew the earth's energy into me, used it, formed it to my will. I concentrated on the central spark, the flame within. I only had to lengthen it, extend what was already there, through my hands. I envisioned the orange, blue, and white light, the heat that made the thing called 'fire.' Sweat poured from my brow. Blood rushed through my veins, and I felt as if I were the flame itself, reaching from earth to sky.

The flame rose from the flagstones and into the air. It hovered, suspended in mid-air, surrounded by an ethereal light. A symbol of the past life I had led and of the power I now possessed.

"Dar, watch." I went to Dun Ailenn to find her. I wanted to explain to her about the perpetual flame before she saw it at the school. We met in the sacred grove next to the stream. I held my hand to a pile of brush and kindling and concentrated on lighting the internal spark. Fire rose easily through me. The kindling caught. Orange flames licked the brush.

"It's Brigid's power," Dar whispered as she watched the flames. "The old Brigid. The Ancient One. She brings the Imbolc light with her fire, she burns the smithy's forge. You've found it."

"Ground yourselves." I waited for my students' breathing to commence in unison. It was their first day and we began with a basic meditation.. "Focus on the flame. Concentrate on its purity." Meditation was a daily practice. They needed to understand silence. They needed to find the earth's energy with all of their senses.

I breathed in my own moment of freedom, relieved to be away from Maithghean's prying eyes and Bacene's harassment. I was free from Elían's spying, free from my father's doubt. The constant watching. The interminable criticisms. I didn't realize how constrained my life had been until I tasted independence.

Messages and rumors reached me. Maithghean spread the word that the school was his idea, that he and Father granted me permission to build it. He inferred I only assisted him as a teacher. Ean laughed when he told me this story. "I didn't disagree with Maithghean when he told me his version of your success. Rest assured we of Dun Ailenn know the truth of who leads the druid school of the Sacred Oak." Ean named it, unintentionally, but it fit. The school of the Sacred Oak.

"We are here to keep our traditions," I said as we greeted our new students. It was only girls who joined.

"They don't trust us yet," Dar grumbled.

I didn't care. I was happy enough students came through our door, with animals and gold as payment for a full year of training. Their ages ranged from about eight to thirteen, all with varying degrees of skill. Some hadn't studied at all. Most accomplished at least one year. A few of the younger girls were homesick, tears still wet on their faces.

"As you know, our people have forgotten the old ways," I said. Nineteen girls nodded. The older ones understood. "We want to re-establish our old beliefs, ground ourselves in them. We can't let our people forget the Ancient Ones who founded this land."

"You'll notice," I added, "everyone who works at the school of the Sacred Oak does so voluntarily. We do not tolerate servitude."

"How?" asked Catha, the daughter of Dun Ailenn's bard.

"We will help the poor. We will offer charity, regardless of their social class. Look around you. We met with many of you at the beginning of summer in your own villages. We accepted many students to this school and not all of you are children of kings or druids."

An uneasy murmur floated through the courtyard. The girls glanced from one to another, wondering who was of a higher or lower status. They couldn't tell. They had no brightly colored skirts. No cloaks of yellow or blue or gray. We'd given them all plain blue robes, woven of the finest flax. For winter, they'd receive robes of warm wool. Dar and I also wore dark blue robes. We asked the Dun Ailenn druids to wear their plainest robes when they came to teach. I refused to show the plaid colors of familial rank at the Sacred Oak, we refused the gold torcs or the carved staffs fitted with bronze. The social hierarchy wouldn't pass through our gates.

"We offer you a new kind of druid training. All of you have potential to be healers or seers or bards. It doesn't matter to whom you were born or in what house you lived. Do you understand this? If you don't," I concluded. "You're free to return to your villages." They wouldn't. It would be an embarrassment to go home without any new knowledge. They were offered something new. All they gained would be returned to their homes. New ideas of change, new ideas to resist change, would spread across the land.

CHAPTER 10

Brigid

Nineteen female acolytes formed a semi-circle around the perpetual flame. I focused on my class before me. "Breathe. Ground. Let the fire speak to you," I said. A surge of pride flowed through me. The gifts blooming under the sacred oak proved it was a place of power. I was blessed with women eager to study nature, art, and the old ways andI had the Danann to help me. As the girls settled into their joined breath, I sat with them to take part in the meditation. I closed my eyes.

The torch of fire floated above us. Although I could use my power to raise it from the copper cauldron, I couldn't answer how it stayed forever lit. I started the fire and lifted it.

The young girls gathered power from the earth, drew it into their bodies. The energy of the students kept it lit. An invisible column of perpetual energy rose up from the earth and held the flame. This is a sacred place. I allowed my mind to wander, to relax, and to eventually empty their minds of thoughts. I tried again...sank to the earth...breathed, waited for Danu to fill me and lead me into vision. I relaxed, I let go.

Brigid, why did you leave me?

I searched through a fog for the voice...

How could you forget?

I didn't forget, I replied. I called for you and you came. We will be victorious.

I turned and Patrick was there, blue eyes piercing through the fog. He reached for me and held me close, as if relieved by my presence. From below, they reached for me. I clung to him.

They will not take you, he said fiercely. Follow me.

I ran with him, struggling against the void that begged me to return to my people. I will not return to you. My place is here. Dagda appeared before me, and I backed away only to find Lugh there. Then Macha. Then Fodla. Come to us, we need your help. The Danann encircled me.

You don't want my help, I said. You want to take what I have worked hard to find.

Please, Brigid. Please help us. They reached for me and I couldn't breathe. They took my breath from me.

Patrick raised his walking staff to strike at them.

"No!" I screamed.

"Brigid? Brigid?" Dar's voice broke through the confusion as I gasped for air. She held my hand. Our students surrounded us, young girls most likely terrified of my screams during their first lesson.

"You were sinking," Dar whispered. I felt the hard flagstones beneath me. They had formed to the shape of my body.

"Go into the main hall," she said quietly to the girls. "Stew and bread have been prepared for you because it's your first day here. Tomorrow, you'll make your own meals."

"Brigid?" asked Catha. "Are you all right?"

I nodded and waved her away.

"After dinner we'll discuss..." Dar interrupted me. "Catha, go to your meal."

Dar lifted me, and I leaned against her as I stumbled toward our shared round house. "You can't discuss this with the girls," she said. "If you can't talk about it with me, you can't talk about it with them. What happened?"

I closed my eyes. My best friend was a seer, a visionary, and could read through my eyes and into my soul.

"Brigid, I hear you call for him in the night." She stroked my brow until I turned to her again.

"Who?" My voice cracked with thirst. She filled a mug with fresh water from the cistern outside our door. I drank it greedily. She took the cup from my hands.

"You dream of him at every full moon. I heard your dreams even when we were at Dun Ailenn. Do you think I've not noticed? You called for him during your meditation tonight as you were, I don't know how else to describe it, sinking into the ground."

I didn't know I had called out his name. I lay back on my bed, exhausted. The pallet, filled with fresh hay, crackled beneath me, and I gave a moment of thanks for its comfort. I had not ever spoken of Patrick, the shepherd boy, my past-life soul mate, to anyone except Elían. He was my secret. I couldn't explain our past in the west, how we discovered the past that tied us both to the very founding of this land.

"My dreams are becoming more powerful," I began hesitantly. "I've had the same dreams all my life."

"Visions aren't easy to explain." Dar understood the intensity of feeling something that no other could experience.

"He's there. He protects me, pulls me away from... something."

I longed for him. Wanted him. A hollow feeling spread through me when I thought of not seeing him ever again.

"What about the stones, Brigid?" asked Dar. "You were melting into them, like something was pulling you down. Did Patrick save you? Just then?"

"It's like the fire. I reach for it and it's there..." I stopped. What I began to say was a lie. Dar wanted the truth. "Patrick always saves me from them. He's the only one who can." She deserved the truth, at least what piece of it I could spare.

CHAPTER 11

Brigid

Then the day came when my father arrived at the school's gates. I had begun to think that Fotharit had forgotten about me. They'd left me alone for seasons. I stood at the gate of the Sacred Oak. If my father were here unaccompanied to see me, I'd let him in. If he were here with druids, I'd have been more fearful. He was alone and wore a plain brown cloak. No marks of a druid on him. No Bacene or Elían or Maithghean to shadow his steps. Still, I motioned for two of Ailenn's warriors to stay at my side.

"You cannot take me from this property. It is Ailenn's land, not yours."

"I don't plan to take you. Dunlang does not want to war with Ailenn." He looked over my shoulder, around the courtyard, and scanned the grounds of the school. Nineteen druids, along with those who wanted to work in freedom, busily formed a thriving community. Dar and several of her students were in the garden, veiled by the lush growth. Fires burned at the smith's workshops, accentuated by loud clangs and flying sparks, creating new metal works.

"Your school is flourishing," Father said, as if he expected the opposite. "But I'm not here to discuss druid craft." I felt his comment was a reference to my slave status. "I wanted to see how you fared after all this time and bring news from home."

I brought him to the sacred flame, perpetual in the courtyard. I wanted him to see the power we possessed, I possessed, without his help. "The school is doing well."

I'd never admit to him any financial concerns. More people, poor, starving people, brought more sheep and goats, but not enough cows to pay Ailenn. More cheese and vegetables were used here to feed our community than sent back to Ean for the druid's portion.

"We have many students," I said. "We will have new druids to initiate to apprentice level soon." Several of the women would be teachers, healers, and seers. Only one, Cecilia, showed the promise of being a bard. Her road of study would last many more years.

"Power over fire is a difficult skill to learn," said Father, watching the flame with the calm demeanor of a druid. He might be surprised by its continuous light, but he'd never admit it.

"We have all learned to tend the flame."

"Can we talk, Brigid? Not here. The oak, perhaps?"

We left the school, with the warriors following. Father's presence there made me uncomfortable. My instinct said not to trust him completely. I didn't know what information he would bring to Maithghean. What he had seen was enough for them to discuss for many days. We sat together under the oak tree, as we had years before, when my extraordinary journey through memories and visions began. The thick branches clustered with green leaves offered us shade from the summer heat. We paid our respects to the sacred oak with ancient druid gestures and then closed our eyes to meditate. I felt a brief rush of good will toward my father as I remembered my girlhood lessons. I sank deeper to the roots of the tree, as he'd taught.

When we settled into ourselves, he spoke. "Brigid, I've another reason for my visit."

"What is it?" I opened my eyes and willed myself to return to the world again.

"We would like to work with you and your school. Fotharit druids. All of us."

I scoffed. This didn't surprise me and I regretted my moments of forgiveness toward Father.

"The druids of Fotharit kidnapped me, enslaved me...why on earth do you think I would want your druids here?"

"You wouldn't have to return to Fotharit, although it is in our right to make you... if you continue to defy me, if you continue to refuse marriage to Tagdh -"

"How does Tagdh feel about all of this? Isn't he humiliated by my constant refusal? And really, Father, shouldn't he ask me himself? I don't think I've had a conversation with him that didn't involve a ritual or ceremonial question." I couldn't help but be sharp at the ridiculousness of it all.

Father closed his eyes, willing his errant child into silence. "As I said before, if you continue to defy *us*, I will invoke the Brehons and transfer your slave status.To Maithghean. And Dunlang will prepare for battle against Dun Ailenn. Tell Ailenn to ready his warriors if that is what you choose."

So if a forced marriage wouldn't work, they would threaten war. The words blurred around me. Alliance, marriage...marriage to Tagdh or slavery under Maithghean or war. I viewed all that surrounded me. This school was mine. I created it. Dar and I, and our students, were responsible for its success. So, there it was. My choice. Marriage to a man I did not know, much less love, or slavery, permanent servitude to a man I detested. Or bloodshed to the innocent people of Dun Ailenn and this school. I waved my hand and the warriors stepped closer.

"Brigid, think of the power you and Tagdh would share teaching here together. This could become the most sought after druid school in the land."

"It's the *only* druid school in the land."

He waved his hand, dismissing my point of the obvious. "Perhaps I was wrong in my approach. Fotharit needs powerful druids. You and Tagdh will help shape them here."

"A marriage to Tagdh or anyone else will not make druids more or less powerful. Why do you have this sudden need for powerful druids? You and Maithghean believed the order was fine. You didn't think there were any weaknesses. You had no problem kicking me out."

"Staying here solves that problem of Maithghean's." He shrugged as if he had nothing to do with that decision. "It is not just the marriage and our alliance, Brigid. Think of how your school could grow with help from your home." Father pressed. "Two druids, this school. It would accomplish everything you have set out to do."

"Two druids? Do you consider me a druid now?"

"Think of the power Fotharit could add to your school."

The union of Patrick and myself would add power to this school. *Patrick, Padraic...* Lightheadedness caught me. I clenched handfuls of grass and soil. Forced myself to the present.

I stood and let the warriors surround me. "Goodbye Father."

I went immediately to Ailenn and told him what Dubhtach had said. "If you want me to leave, I will. I don't want to be responsible for a war between our tribes."

We sat in his meeting hall alone, no Ean, no Dar. I only brought the warriors who had been with me, to verify what had been said.

Ailenn rubbed his broad forehead with his hand, weighing his options. "Obviously, I don't want a battle, not now with the hunger as it is. And to be honest Brigid, your school - as Ean predicted - has brought much success and fame to Dun Ailenn. One chief druid asked that his student stay here to finish her training. Completely. Celia, is it?"

This news surprised and pleased me. I nodded and Ailenn continued. "Their bard is sickly and can't provide what she needs. But he will send others from her tribe to help with the histories and what not." He lifted his head from his hands. "So, you leaving does not help either. I suspect the threat of battle is a ruse. Dunlang has as many starving cattle as we do. And while you are a guest on my land, that won't last forever. Giving you to Maithghean is particularly underhanded."

He motioned to the warriors to join us and Ean appeared from the shadows. I thought we had been alone. "This is what I propose," said Ailenn. "You and Dar travel up the coast as planned to bring in more students. The warriors will accompany you. With my daughter and my men, you still cannot be taken by Fotharit, at least not legally, if it comes to that. Alone is a different story. You and Dar recruit more students. My two best swordsmen here will recruit tribes to our side, to fight with us if needed. For now, talk only," he warned the men. "If it does come to battle, I want to know who is on our side, and who is capable of being on our side. If everyone is famished and crops are poor, there will be no fighting. Not over Maithghean's obsessions and not over a girl."

CHAPTER 12

Brigid

Dar and I walked north in early spring, to talk to druids about our school. Guards followed behind us. There was a chill in the air and mud on the roads but we were hopeful that this next year would be a clear success. We were welcomed as guests in villages and forts, and for the most part, druids listened to our stories about the school of the Sacred Oak.

"We've been waiting to hear about the Sacred Oak school," said Conor, a druid who had visited my home when I was a child. He took us in from the damp mist.

"It has a solid foundation and continues to grow," I said. This time, we sat in front of his hearth, our blue cloaks drying on a bench, near the fire. I saw him glance at our cloaks, looking for the druid plaid.

"We'll be adding our third class," Dar said. "One focus of our teaching is to accept all who choose to learn, not only those appointed by their druids.

Conor's brows lifted as he offered both of us ale. I took it out of politeness, sipping slowly. "And not train in their home? What about their histories? Their genealogies?" he asked.

Dar explained the agreement we had with Celia's chief druid. Bards from her tribe were visiting teachers and taught her individually. Others on the bard-path could join to analyze techniques though, obviously, the content was not their own. These visiting bards were with the students now.

Conor mulled this over. "I'll speak to the order tomorrow. I doubt we'd send all of our acolytes. We have three in training now but one young girl - she has the interest but not the birthright - might benefit from your healing tutelage, Brigid."

Dar and I caught eyes and smiled. It was working. Our school would grow and continue. And then Conor shared a story with us that changed everything.

"Another thing to consider as you gather acolytes to you," Conor set his mug under the spout of the cider barrel to refill his cup. "Is this new wave of Christians living among us."

"My mother lives among the Palladians. They are a small community, peaceable," I said.

"Peaceable, yes. But there's a new one among them. He wanders around the land, speaking of their faith. Travels from village to village even though the Church has set him up with a place in the north. More than one person here has shown interest, and truth be told, it has me a little concerned."

"Wait," said Dar. She knew what Conor was going to say. She took my hand in hers, as if to prepare me for bad news. But Conor, five or six pints in, didn't notice her warning.

"Now, a few in my village talk of the one god," said Conor. "But those who do follow this man are very fervent. They speak of a new priest who gathers larger crowds than Palladius ever did. They asked permission to leave here and to follow him. Since we're in the midst of a famine, there's less food to share and no crops to tend, so the chieftain let them go. Fewer mouths to feed, as far as he is concerned. Now, they're off to find this man."

"Who is he?" I asked. For some reason, I was thinking Erc, or my uncle Cormac, perhaps, had taken to the hills to bring people to their community.

"Patrick. He's a Briton but says he was a shepherd in the western hills years ago. The women seem to like him, especially warriors' widows."

I jumped as if set on fire. Patrick. He was here. It had to be him. It had to be. My heart raced and Dar kept my hand in hers. Her grasp kept me from running out the door in search of him.

"Brigid?" Conor glanced at me.

"I'm fine. A cinder, I think." I brushed at my skirt and pretended to search for errant embers.

"So why the warriors' widows in particular?" asked Dar.

Conor took another long swallow from his mug of ale and belched. "Their one god has a son they call Jesus and a wife, Mary. Jesus is a peaceable type, so the women follow. Women are tired of seeing their men slain."

"So a few widows find their peace. I don't see a cause for concern." Dar's words were casual but I could hear a tightness in her tone.

"Neither do I. Not really. Except for Patrick seems to talk often about the end of slavery, that all are equal in the eyes of his god. His words give slaves hope."

Dar made a small sound in her throat and uneasiness pervaded the room. "That's our goal," she said. "We teach our students to live without slaves, without captives of war."

Conor poured himself more ale. He offered us another mug but Dar and I shook our heads. "Your school may have some competition among the slaves. I hear, Brigid, that your mother Brocca is a strong supporter of Patrick."

Later, when I went to the guest house, I let my thoughts crash into one another. "I don't want to talk," I said to Dar. "Let me think and I will explain it all tomorrow."

Patrick. Alive. Here. I wanted to run to him, to see him, to hold him in my arms again. But he wasn't the same. He was preaching the Christian belief. Patrick's religion. It always had been as much as Dathi and I tried to convince him otherwise. Christians and their God and his son. It didn't matter. I had to see him. I wanted to tell him why I didn't return, tell him that the school was evolved from Dathi's idea. Patrick could help, I was sure of it. I recalled the past with the Danann more every day. Surely he must remember too.

I finally shared the story of Patrick with my friend. I couldn't hide it from Dar any longer. I didn't know why I was hiding my past with Patrick at all; I'd gotten used to keeping secrets from Maithghean and it seemed to be a hard habit to break. "The Test of the Ancients opened a door. I didn't remember everything all at once. I still don't. Memories, flashes come here and there. When Dathi introduced me to Patrick, he was a shepherd, kidnapped by raiders from Britannia. But I *knew* him."

"And did he know you?" she asked. We walked north, to the ring fort Conor had described.

"He did but can't admit it. Wouldn't admit it. He's born and raised Christian. He never trusted the druids. He did gain some memories. Dreams, he called them, not memories. But he was part of this plan, our school, everything Dathi and I imagined for Éire.

"And...there's more to it?"

This was the problem with having a friend who was clairvoyant.I nodded, sure the warriors were listening in to every bit of our conversation. What did it matter? I needed to practice living a life without secrets, at least at Dun Ailenn. "We loved each other. We made plans to escape, so he could return to Britannia and I could work with druids there. I was so concerned with earning my rank. I waited for Dathi and Raven to bestow it on me, to make me part of their order - which they never did. And then I was taken away, kidnapped by Maithghean. Patrick was left alone on the hillside and I don't know what happened to him."

"That's why you had Father send the messengers overseas."

"Yes, and even before then I'd sent some secretly from Fotharit. Patrick was gone. He wasn't in the west and no one could find him in his hometown."

I allowed my worrisome thoughts to crash around. What if it wasn't him? There's bound to be more than one Patrick in the world but one who was a shepherd? Kidnapped into slavery? I knew it was him. I just knew.

As the sun shifted past noon, we approached a village with a gathering of people outside the fort gates. They seemed to be farmers. Servants. Plain skirts and cloaks. No plaid. No nobility or gold torcs that I could see. We stayed on the outside of the crowd and I pulled my blue cloak and hood close.

Patrick stepped onto a mound and began to speak. I heard their whispers of the people. *He was a shepherd years ago. He escaped, and now returned.*

It was him. My heart raced. He wore long robes, a plain brown and blue, with a wooden carved cross for a necklace.I stayed hidden in the shadows, in the back of the crowd; my cloak covered me. Dar stood by my side. I needed her strength.

"Jesus Christ, the son of God." People quieted to hear his strong but temperate voice. "The son of God shines his light upon you, as the fabled Lugh shines his light, as he was the son of the Sun."

I cringed. Fabled?

"Jesus," he continued, "was a poor man like you, but blessed as the son of the Virgin Mary, as the children of Eiru were blessed."

I bristled again as he used the names of my people – *our* people – my family of the past, the founders of this very island. He was using the old Gods to put forth his Christian message so that the simple folk would listen to his words about this 'Jesus.' How could he compare this peasant man from distant, dusty Israel to the gods of our lush green isle?

Anger surged from the earth through the soles of my feet. Anger overrode love, overrode longing. It washed over me, through me, warmth that began with the earth under my feet, slowly spreading upwards. My control was lost to that of the goddess who filled me.

He combined his Christian stories with the Ancient Ones, merging them together. He skillfully wove a connection between the ancient gods of Ireland and his new God, shared by the Romans. "The gods of this land accepted the love of Christ. The Dagda turned to the Lord when all else failed."

That was it. How dare he describe Dagda as a Christian? My brow was hot with fury and my forehead pulsed. I pushed forward to the front of the crowd. "No! Your stories are not true!"

"Brigid." A silence descended as the villagers followed Patrick's gaze toward me. He swallowed hard. "I looked for you. I went to Fotharit. But you left. They didn't know where."

I ignored his words for now. "How dare you?" I marched to the foot of the mound. My rage carried me forward. "How dare you tell lies about the Ancient Ones?"

Dar grabbed my arm, but I threw her off. The group began to whisper. "Who is she?" they murmured amongst themselves.

"I speak only the word of God." His voice wavered and cracked like a young boy's.

"You speak the words of the Christians! And you use the gods of the Irish to do so. This is wrong!" All that Dathi had taught him. All that I had taught him in Foclut Forest. From his height on the mound, his blue eyes looked down and locked with mine.

"You promised to return," he whispered. "Brigid? You promised. And you left me alone."

The puzzlement on my face matched his. Frustration welled within me. Dathi never told him of my kidnapping. I felt sick. He never knew. Patrick thought all these years that I had left him willingly.

I took a deep breath and stayed focused on my mission. "You promised to speak about the Danann," I said. His blue gaze met mine. Penetrated into my very soul.

"Did I promise that?" He stood taller when he realized I wouldn't answer his charge of being left alone. "If so, I believe I have mentioned the Old Ones of Éire often." He pitched his voice so the crowd around him heard.

"You've twisted it to your own advantage." I was furious. His words wouldn't help the Danann return. It would only entice people to join the Christians because they recognized the Irish legend. My body trembled with energy and power that was not my own. I felt the pulse that accompanied the Test, the memories that came from it. I wanted to lash out at him, to make him repeat his promise, yet I knew with so many years behind us when he was left alone, I was at a disadvantage. Slowly, Patrick walked down the slope to my side and reached out to me. I trembled, wanting to pull him close, but so angry at what he'd become. He touched my blue cloak and traced the hood. Strong fingers brushed past my face. I closed my eyes, wishing to the depths of the earth for the strength to pull away.

I couldn't. I turned toward him and rested the side of my face in his hand. His hand fit me perfectly as if my shape was meant to match his. Silence surrounded us. Only the purest energy flowed between us, the kind of strength that flowed from the earth. I opened my eyes and found his eyes closed, while a tear traced its way past his thick eyelashes. Patrick and I remained cocooned in a silent world of our own.

A spark snapped and singed the threads of my cloak. Wisps of smoke curled around my face. We both jumped back. A cold panic overwhelmed me. Our eyes held as I backed away through the throng of people.

"Brigid, wait..." Patrick held up his hand, his fingers blackened with soot.

I pushed my Dar toward the road, ignoring her questions as I ran, with the warriors following us. I glanced back only once to see Patrick run toward me, then pause, held back by the crowd that encircled him.

CHAPTER 13

Brigid

The noise of horse hooves interrupted my class's study of fire in the courtyard. The novices scrambled up from their seated positions beneath the flame, startled as much as I by the disruption.

A small man, dressed in robes similar to Patrick's, dismounted his horse and several other men trailed behind him.

"I'm Bishop Mel," he said. "Brocca said we could find you here."

I introduced the Christian man to my students. The commotion sufficiently ended the lesson, and we would have to save the continued mystery of the flame for another day. The girls gathered around me and stared wide-eyed at the brown-robed Christians. They were men and women, former slaves and servants. The druid girls stared because they hadn't met many of their people who converted.

"He is a friend of my mother," I said to my class "Bishop Mel, these are my students. All are druids in training. Girls, bring us water. These travelers are tired and thirsty. Then help the cook prepare bread and cheese for a feast."

I dismissed the girls and turned to our visitors, leading them to benches in the courtyard. "Mel, do you bring news of my mother?"

"She is doing well and is happy. She wished for me to visit you. From what she's told me, I believe you are blessed by the Lord and He is calling you to Him." Mel was serious.

I laughed. "I seriously doubt the Lord is calling me. I'm a druid, Mel. I don't believe in the Christian faith and their determination to wash away all other beliefs." I thought of how Patrick bent the truth.

"Not all Christians are as determined as that," Mel said. "I myself enjoy debating theology with the druids and always look for common ground." I shivered with a brief trace of foresight. Not all of his persuasion would be so open to debate. "I thought you might have an interest since your mother converted. I've heard from Erc she is an asset to their community."

"Bishop Mel, I have no interest in changing my beliefs. We built this school to strengthen druid work. My mother knows this."

"Your work here is gaining a reputation up and down the coast," he said. "We've heard of the help you've given the poor here. We know you hate slavery as much as we do. We really do have similar missions. And I've heard about the threats from Fotharit."

Bishop Mel hadn't come here for a friendly visit on my mother's behalf. There was something else. The threats had continued and Ailenn began battle drills with his warriors.

"Think of all the people you could help alongside the Christians," he said. "Here. At this school."

"Alongside the Christians?" The sunlight grew dim, and the branches of the oak rustled in the breeze.

"I'm afraid I stated that a little too bluntly. Let me rephrase. Think of this school as a *partnership with* our church, rather than *part of*. Is that better?"

I shook my head, still confused. His proposal made no sense. "Why do you want to partner with druids?"

He shifted his position on the wooden bench as he explained. "Consider it a dual center of learning, for both Christian and druid. With funding from the church, we could expand, send out missionaries, and show the people of Éire that coexistence is possible."

"Mel, the idea of coexistence is all very nice. There is more to it, isn't there?" As Mel explained his vision, my mind raced. Patrick. A place where Christian and druid learned together meant Patrick would have to be involved somehow, in some way. I focused on Mel again. The church wanted what we had: the land, the well-traveled road nearby, the water source, the converts.

"You want the people we bring in," I said. "You've seen our success. Fewer freed slaves, fewer of the poor and hungry, have gone to Erc's village. They've come here instead. You want access to those people."

"Let's put it this way, Brigid. We'd like to share the space. We don't want to take it from you. We'd build our own housing, our church on the east side of the land. Let those who come here decide which side to choose."

The east side. Closest to the road. "Even if I agree with your plan, I can't give you permission to build here. This land is loaned to us by Ailenn. It would be Ailenn's decision. Not mine." Bishop Mel was paying me a courtesy.

He cleared his throat. My guess was that he and Ailenn had already settled this proposal. "The Church will buy the land, all of it. It would ease your financial burdens, erase them completely, and you could operate your school as you see fit."

"Do you know how much this would cost? There aren't enough cows in Éire."

"The Church is paying for it. We will share it, Brigid, and you have no more debt to Ailenn."

I couldn't imagine such wealth. The Christians were more powerful than I cared to admit. I leaned back on the bench to think. If the Church would pay off the debt, and all we had to do was share a field, far on the other side... "Bishop Mel, then my school would be owned by the Christians. We might share some of the same goals when it comes to slavery but our students come here to study the druid arts, to remember the history and religion of our people. We don't want to be converted."

"No, no," Mel said. "We will not try to convert your students already here. No conversions, at least not outright. If your people choose to visit us, we will, of course, welcome them."

I let his words sink in. Free of debt. All we'd have to do is share the land. He explained in more detail that one of his priests, Conleth, would lead the Christian community.

"Really," said Mel, "Ailenn isn't going to turn down the scores of cows and gold we will give him." The interesting part, and his face lit up as he spoke of it, was that the monastery would serve men and women, nuns and monks. "Until we become established, I would need your help administering the women's side of things, but simply in the realm of administration, arranging the housing and dormitories."

"You're asking me to run your monastery? Along with my school?"

He grinned sheepishly. "Just the set up for the women's housing and supplies. This isn't something appropriate for Conleth. We will be recruiting new nuns. We don't have many women in our order, not yet. A temporary thing until we are running smoothly. You would be compensated, of course. Let me know what supplies you need and we'll order them for you."

"Supplies? How about food? Cows? A new barn built just for dairy? A quern for grain?" I had a long list of things that our growing community still needed.

"You will have no other ties to the church, Brigid. I promise. Be good neighbors to us; that is all. Help us with the setup and organization."

"You make a tempting offer. We'd be happy to be free of debt to Ailenn. But the land would belong to the church. What if you decided to take it all? Where would we go?"

"This is my parish, Brigid. My domain. Your mother is my friend and one of my converts. I wouldn't betray her or you. You would have to trust that as long as we are here on this land, so are you."

I took a deep breath and brought up my final argument to Bishop Mel. "My father and Maithghean could come to our gates at the next full moon," I said. "I need the promise of your protection."

"Their words have no effect on Church property. They are outside of their villages. This appeals to Ailenn. He receives payment and doesn't have to battle anyone for it. Chieftains will have no power here."

I breathed a sigh of relief. The old rules of battles and raids would not work. The rules about slavery would not work. I was thankful my mother sent Bishop Mel to me. She knew I needed a way out of the Law. And an alliance with the Christians...I couldn't help it. *Patrick.*

CHAPTER 14

Brigid

In harmony, the druids and students performed the sunset ritual. We bid farewell to the sun as we faced west. We raised our arms and then lowered them, sinking in unison with the orange light. West always called to me, and I envisioned its oak forests and rocky coast. The ritual ended and we meditated into the evening in the late spring warmth. I let the meditation run longer than usual before I broke the news to my students, nineteen young women bundled in their blue wool cloaks, copper brooches shining in the last of the sun's rays. They formed their usual circle around the flame.

"You know the difficult decision that has been set before us," I began quietly. "There are many paths our school may take. I know there are many fears that accompany any changes."

"Why do we have to change at all?" Catha had the soft-spoken voice of a sparrow.

"We depend on our neighbors from Dun Ailenn for many supplies, but especially protection. They will help, but they will not go to battle with Fotharit over me, nor do I expect them to," I said. "We can manage our gardening, shepherding, and weaving, but we are still young and still dependent. Maithghean sees our weakness as his advantage. He will offer Fotharit's support. The Christians, on the other hand, offer us a way to continue what we are doing, albeit an odd situation."

I watched as the druid acolytes looked to one another in an exchange of worried glances. I took a deep breath and continued. "If I refuse the Bishop's offer, then I will have to marry Tagdh, Maithghean would most likely take over your training, and the school would effectively be ruled by the druids in Fotharit."

"Why should we all have to pay the price for your personal situation? Why should we give up our freedom because you don't want to marry?" an irritable Cecilia called out.

"I could leave, if that would make you happy, Cecilia, or perhaps you may compose a satire against me as you study bardcraft." I couldn't help but to edge my comment with sarcasm. I looked each acolyte in the eye. Cecilia blushed and allowed her long brown hair to cover her face.

"If you want Maithghean and the Fotharit druids to lead you instead, that is your choice. That is what we are here to discuss. He is a powerful chief druid, and no one from Dun Ailenn will contest him, not even Ean."

Dar stood beside me as I put my leadership on the line. The final choice would be made by the students. "If it is your choice, as Cecilia suggested, I will return to Fotharit to do my father's bidding, so the school will remain a completely druid college, under Maithghean's direction." There were murmurs of dissent, and I waited until the voices quieted. Maithghean's reputation for dark sorcery was well known.

"However, if we accept Bishop Mel's offer and allow Christian nuns and monks to live alongside us, nothing would change for you. You will continue your studies as you are now and perhaps learn something new from the Christians."

"I think many students are wondering if the Christian influence will be greater than Maithghean's," Dar's soft voice resonated.

"That will be our challenge," I admitted. "Patrick, one of their priests, uses our old gods to make comparisons with theirs." I swallowed hard after saying his name. "It makes a switch in belief easy. To be fair, not all of the priests do this." Next, I explained I wouldn't be changing my beliefs or my teachings, though some outsiders might believe I was a Christian abbess because of the new responsibilities I would take on. To honor Mel's request, we couldn't tell them otherwise.

"Isn't our purpose to fight the Christians?" Cecilia brought us back to our serious topic. Her voice lost its sharp edge. She practiced the art of song and satire and, like Bacene, created a few directed toward the brown-robed monks that visited.

"I don't know if *fight* is the word we want to use. How do we war with them directly? Many of our people are Christians. My own mother converted. Their goal is one of peace and freedom. I have no quarrel with that. Our goal is not to force people to believe one thing or another, but to ensure that our people remember their own history, our ancient gods." I was being gracious, generous with the Christians. As much as I found fault with Patrick's methods, I needed their protection, pure and simple. "Our goal is to strengthen our túaths by practicing what the Danann taught us. We need everyone to recognize the Danann gods and goddesses."

In the end, all the girls stayed.

Bishop Mel sent in monks to begin building lodges for the Christians who would join us. The neighboring hillside was full of whitewash, thatch, and men. They eyed the druid novices carefully, and the druid acolytes watched them. "Leave the monks to their work," I said and sent the girls back to their studies. I'd given Mel my word that there would be no theological arguments between the two sides.

It was close to the winter solstice when the first Christian nuns and monks settled into their new homes on the grounds of the sacred oak. Instead of seeing the timing as a bad omen, I decided the end of the season's wheel would have a positive outlook. It was time to end the old. Dar and I planned the ceremony to reflect acceptance of change. The clouds parted and the sun glanced off the frost that edged the reddened leaves of the oak. The nuns in their dark robes didn't look very different from the druids. I greeted them in the courtyard.

"We want you to study and worship as you wish. I will provide instruction for those of you interested in healing. Dar will work with you in the gardens." Many of the plants grown were to help her in her seer-work. It would be up to the monks and nuns to decide if they wanted seer-work.

I indicated to my right where Mariah, the lead nun, sat. We met in the preceding weeks and came to a tentative agreement on how to organize our respective lessons and apprenticeships. She was the one who refused this administrative position. "Mariah will teach the Christian rites, reading, and writing in one of the new buildings. I believe they will also have a room for music."

Cecilia gasped at the word 'writing.'

Catha raised her hand. "Brigid, I'm studying music and the harp. Am I permitted to observe a Christian music class?" Her eyes were eager. She wanted to learn to write, as well as memorize the poems and lyrics she learned. The differences had already begun, and I would need to figure out how to straddle both of these worlds.

"This is a place of learning. However, you should ask permission from your chief druid in your home túath before participating in something that may be detrimental to your initiation."

Dar chimed in. "Christian nuns are welcome at our public rituals. Of course, there are many aspects of our training that we may not share."

I turned to Mariah, a tall thin woman from the North. Patrick's country. "Do you agree? Can the druid women learn from the Christian nuns?"

She nodded. "However, I ask that any nun receive my permission before attending any druid ceremony."

Since most of the nuns were from Eire, I wondered why they would need permission to attend ceremonies they had most witnessed their entire lives. Yet, they were glowing, ethereal. Their faith was strong and borne of conviction, despite past enslavement.

I questioned Mariah as the women went to the kitchen to prepare the evening meal. She chose to come here, instead of Armagh.

"I'd love to stay in Armagh, but it was limited for the nuns."

"What was limited?"

"The classes, the opportunities. I can read and write a little, but I want to work with illumination," said Mariah. There was that word again, the unfamiliar one. I couldn't read or write at all. I could tell stories of generations, all from memory. "Here, there are more opportunities for different studies."

"So, you don't want to run the nunnery?" I hoped, with one last chance, Mariah would want to take over the administrative role I had agreed to fill.

"Why do you think that? I want a quiet room where I can read, write, and illustrate for the Lord."

"Tell me of the mission at Armagh. Why couldn't you do these things there?" I hoped my interest was not overly apparent.

"Well, it's just so crowded. Every priest in Éire, and some from the British Isle, has heard of Patrick and they want to study with him. They get the first choice of the classes. There's not much space left for the nuns, although Patrick has tried. He appointed new teachers, but still...there was no space."

Patrick. He was in Armagh, far north.

I took a deep breath and steadied my words. "Why is Patrick so popular?" I knew why. I'd heard him speak. I was curious as to what she would say.

Mariah brightened. "Patrick has a presence that brings us all together. To hear him speak is a gift. You must witness his sermons."

"I was a witness, Mariah, many years ago."

CHAPTER 15

Brigid

The fury of the Fotharit druids charged the sky with energy. Maithghean's anger shot like a lightning bolt . It was two days past Beltane, and, as promised, the druids of Fotharit came for me.

Warriors had stopped them at the gates, informing them they were on Church property.

"What has possessed you, girl?" Maithghean brimmed with hostility as I met the Fotharit contingent at the entrance. Father refused to meet my eye. Tagdh and Bacene gasped at the sight of monks and nuns in the distance as they strolled to their chapel, built with thatch and whitewash, while druid novices meditated under the Sacred Oak.

"You're no Christian," Maithghean spat.

"I found an alliance necessary." I steadied my voice.

"An alliance?"

"This isn't Dun Ailenn's land. Not anymore. It's not mine, either."

Maithghean looked at Father then back at me.

"You haven't visited the fort yet?" I asked. I feigned innocence. "Ean hasn't shared the news with you?" Although Ean would not fight Maithghean directly, he certainly enjoyed his own form of subterfuge. He had not told Maithghean about the land sale to the Church.

"You're a druid. An apprentice, anyway. Even without all of your past hysterics, I don't see why you would partner with the Christians," said Maithghean.

"I'm a druid apprentice? Really? I thought I was a slave." I looked to my father, but he kept his gaze straight ahead on the flame in the courtyard. "It's worked well, so far. We teach our students, we share a garden, and share our meals. That is all."

"You hold no weight here." I addressed their motive for coming. "This is property of the Church, and you may not take me from it. Chieftain rules and slavery does not apply here."

"We can't take you from it?" Maithghean asked as if he didn't believe the claim.

A warrior guarded the gates, a man from Dun Ailenn. He gripped his sword and glanced at me. I shook my head slightly. Dar appeared, along with several monks, to whom she had apparently explained the Fotharit situation.

"If you take her," the monk explained. "Or anyone on Church grounds, you will have the soldiers of the Roman Empire at your gates. They've had no need to come to this island. Don't give them one."

We, the druids, the monks, and a guard, formed an odd but threatening coalition. We watched as Maithghean's resolve faltered momentarily.

"We don't want to take you, Brigid," Tagdh said. "We came to see your school." Was it possible he had no idea of their plan? Did he know they used his proposal of marriage as a threat?

"Will you deny us?" Bacene snidely referred to the requirement of hospitality. Without a word, Dar and the monks led the druids from Fotharit to the main hall to refresh themselves with food and water. Instead of joining them, Maithghean followed me to the courtyard. I beckoned for the warrior to guard my side as I inspected the flame.

"Leave me be." I spun around to face Maithghean.

"You gave in." He smiled, as if happy for my weakness. "You wanted to bring back the old gods and now look at you with the Christians; you're practically one of them."

"I didn't give in," I said. "I don't share their beliefs, and none of my novice druids have converted to their side."

"You're not the only one who can speak to the Ancient Ones now."

A chill went down my spine. "Did you connect with them? Who? How?"

He ignored my questions. "You've been rebellious ever since your...trip west. Ever since you met Patrick."

I kept my expression immobile when he mentioned Patrick. Maithghean's knowledge scared me. "Is an alliance all this is? You teach druid acolytes by day and share your supper with monks by night?" His yellow eyes lit with an idea. "Perhaps you are trying to influence them, instead of the other way around. Perhaps you are trying to get closer to their leader. Is that your goal, Brigid?" He circled around me, making guesses at my intentions. "Why, Brigid? Why befriend the Christians? To manipulate your way into Patrick's life?"

I was sickened by him, but unable to leave. He continued his circle around me. Like a spider, he wound his way around me. He wove lines of energy that bound us together. Before I could resist, the power of a spell surrounded me. I'd fallen into his trap, even with the warrior next to me. The guard stood dazed and unblinking. How did Maithghean manage to put the guard under his spell, into a trance?

"Ah, all of these sacrifices for Éire? Giving up your beliefs and your pride?" He shook his head. "No, these sacrifices are for him. For Patrick. Padraic," he said in the Irish. "*Padraic*."

"That's enough," I hissed. "The Church cleared my debt. That is all."

"I met Patrick once." Maithghean tapped his fingertips together, one hand against the other, as if beginning a friendly conversation. "He came to Fotharit looking for you. He stayed for a few days. A hurt ankle, it seems, and he asked for you. You, of course, had run away here. Too bad...He also asked if we had warriors to spare. It seems he needs his own guards, like you, for protection in some parts." Maithghean inclined his head toward my guard, who did nothing but stare forward in a daze.

My jaw clenched and I stepped back, breaking his well-drawn web. Patrick had told me as much that day on the mound.

"He has a lot of power, doesn't he?" A shadow brushed his face, created by his own magic.

"Enough, Maithghean," I stressed his name, forcing him to shake the spell and return to the present. "I refuse to hear any more."

I stalked past the magician. I reached to the guard, to awaken him as I passed, but Maithghean seized my arm. I cried out in pain.

"You're a servant, my servant, my slave," he hissed. "Dubhtach agreed. As a matter of fact, he relinquished his rights to you and gave your services to me."

"You're lying."

He bought your mother the same way, a voice inside me flickered. *She was a slave, a prisoner of a pirate's raid. Why wouldn't he do the same to you?* Father had carried through on his threat.

As if my thoughts reached him, Father appeared in the courtyard.

"Is it true?" I demanded. Maithghean tightened his hold on my arm, pinching and twisting.

Father lowered his eyes to the ground. "I wanted to tell you before Maithghean did. I warned you, Brigid, when I visited here last. The Brehons took you from me and now you belong to Maithghean."

Futility rooted itself in the core of my being. Maithghean's slave? I was so attuned to the law of the Brehons, to follow it exactly, that I forgot my surroundings. My father was the ultimate traitor. Maithghean, I knew, would do what he could to crush me. I never doubted otherwise. I believed in Father's goodness. I believed in the man who taught me to summon energy from rocks, who gave me a special wink during Imbolc ceremonies. That man ceased to exist for me. As of that moment, in the courtyard by the flame, Dubhtach of Fotharit was no longer my father.

I drew myself up, harnessing all the magic I could from the elements: air, earth, water, and sun. The Danann moved beneath me. They were on my side. They fought against Maithghean as much as I did. I forced a burst of energy to the dazed warrior so he could shake off Maithghean's spell. "In Fotharit, my status may be revoked." I wrenched my arm painfully from his sharp grasp. His fingernails scratched my skin. "Not here. Not at the Church, not at the Sacred Oak." The warrior held a spear tip to Maithghean's throat. I met his hideous yellow eyes. "You have no power in this land. Leave."

CHAPTER 16

Brigid

Bishop Mel rode his mule westward toward the Hill of Unisech. Travelers told us about the poor crops in the midlands. We'd survived a hard season and wanted to help. Dar and I followed with a mule who pulled his usual wagon. We carried supplies in the wagon in order to help the monks there feed the poor. Mariah and several other nuns joined us on the journey. All of us were unsure if the Christian leaders in Unisech would accept Dar and me, the druid presence.

"You must come," Bishop Mel had insisted. "You know how to deal with large numbers of people, with hungry children. These young monks don't. They're new to the order. Unisech is a new monastery, and the famine has hit hard. You know...well, how to make the food last." He referred to my doubling of bacon and pigs, my father's trick with numbers.

Three new students entered the druid school in the past season. Our Christian neighbors didn't dissuade them, and I believed the odd pairing added to the attraction of the school. Prosperity remained a distant goal, and what little excess we had, we often gave away to those who needed it more. The school by the oak was known for its charitable works, which is why Mel asked for our help in Unisech.

Mel slowed so my old mule, Clover , would catch up. I named the beast Clover because he'd always stop and eat a patch of the greens whenever he could. "Brigid, we are blessed to have you assist the Order. We're grateful for your charity."

"We'll help in any way we can."

"So many knocked at their doors; the monks were overrun with beggars. They have little idea how to organize these things. They gave away most of their supplies and had to ask for donations from Armagh. You know how to economize what you share."

"Brother Ailbe, meet our sisters, Brigid, Darlughdacha, and Mariah." The young man was barely a teenager. Dar and I glanced at each other and then at Mel. Brother Ailbe shook our hands and Dar grinned. We both found it laughable when we were introduced as nuns. Mariah's face stayed immobile. She did not find the duplicity amusing.

"They are from the church...Cill..." Mel fumbled. We all realized we had not given the school or church, nor the combination of the two, a formal name.

"Dara," I finished. "The oak." Cill Dara. Church of the Oak.

We followed Mel inside, curious. Bright whitewash and a thatched roof rose from the dreariness of the shadowy bog. The idea of worshiping inside a building was utterly unfamiliar to Dar and me. Oak trees, tall and strong, surrounded the church. One grew from the center of the room and through the thatched roof. Their wisdom poured through me.

"Dar," I whispered. "Do you feel it?"

"The energy is strong here," she agreed. "A good sign."

The interior of the chapel was rich and earthy, created of oak and rowan wood. Bishop Mel smiled, pleased to see I was enchanted with the place.

"I never knew a church could hold such beauty." I stared in wonder. This little church seemed to be of the trees, as if the oaks built the church themselves. Dar pointed straight ahead. Carved in wood at the altar was the Mother Goddess. I looked closer, questioning if I had missed an important tenet of Christianity. No, not the goddess, I corrected myself upon closer inspection of the carving, not Danu, or the other goddesses of Éire.

"It is the Virgin Mary, Mother of Christ," Mel told me. The actual figure, so similar to the goddesses that guarded the archway at the school, was unnerving. I took a deep breath. The minor delineation in name didn't matter. Her physical presence soothed me. Danu, earth goddess.

"Mariah, let's go and help Brother Ailbe set up his kitchen. Brigid and Dar will join us in a moment," Bishop Mel spoke softly, as if he sensed my need for quiet.

I focused on the sculpture, recognizing the synthesis of beliefs it held. We could work together.

Mel drank red wine as we made our arrangements for handing out stew and bread. We'd brought supplies for the hungry in the western lands hit hard by famine. Brother Ailbe eyed Mel's intake of wine and looked at his colleague doubtfully. I thought of all the wine and ale he'd drank while at Dun Ailenn. Mel's fondness for alcohol was well known.

The monks led us to another building behind the chapel, where pots of mutton stew boiled and wooden bowls lined the several long tabletops. Ailbe introduced us to Declan, a monk in charge of the food preparation. He'd gladly taken our donations and made quick work of the mutton we'd brought. The aroma of spiced meat was tantalizing. Declan stirred the stew and smiled at us, happy with his task.

Women and children from Unisech filled the hall. The men came later, slowly, seemingly embarrassed for their inability to provide for their families. It wasn't their fault. Drought settled into this land. Gardens were dry. Livestock malnourished. Wild game had been depleted from over-hunting. Dar and I set the brothers to work chopping more vegetables for another pot of stew. Mariah baked fresh loaves of bread. When the stew ran out, we found dried venison in the monastery storage. Dar promised Declan she would hunt a deer in our land to replace what was taken. She was quick with the bow and arrow.

"Thank you," one thin woman said as I brought another loaf of bread to her table. "We ate the last of our meat a fortnight ago." The family's milk cow, I guessed. So now they were without meat, cheese, and milk.

"How does your livestock fare?" I asked Brother Ailbe in the kitchen.

"Fine, for now. Much of our cattle and sheep are donations from Armagh."

Armagh. Patrick. I closed my eyes. He helped these people, too. Connected. We were always connected. Brother Ailbe cleared his throat, and I returned to our conversation. "Even more reason for the monastery to donate one of your own," I said.

"Donate?" Bishop Mel joined our conversation. He had, temporarily, set down his wine cup and ladled stew into bowls.

"Do you want followers or not? Share with the tribe. If the drought continues for another moon, your cow will die here as much as it will in their village. Show your generosity." I couldn't believe I was giving them advice on bringing the local Irish to their church, but the monastery had food to share. The village was hungry.

"The cow will show our faith in God," Brother Ailbe added, excited about his idea. "It will symbolize our faith that God will end the drought."

Brother Ailbe led from the stable a large red cow, udders full of milk. "The Brothers of Unisech would like to present this cow to our neighbors. You've provided us with protection. You've welcomed us to your land. We have faith in the Lord, and we believe this hungry time will end soon. Take this animal as a symbol of our faith."

He handed the rope to the chieftain, and the cow ambled westward with the tribe as they headed home.

"Thank you, Brigid," Bishop Mel whispered behind me. "Your generosity has helped us once again."

CHAPTER 17

Brigid

That night, as we settled into the guesthouse, I wondered *why* the village turned to the monastery for help. Dar and I sat in front of the hearth wrapped in our cloaks. Warm embers glowed, taking the chill from the misty night.

"Where were the druids of their tribe?" I asked Dar. They were noticeably absent from the shared meal at the monastery.

"Where were they? What rituals had they done? What predictions of rain and sun had they made?"

"What have the druids done to show their faith the drought would end?" I asked. "Did they share from the druid portions? I don't know."

Dar stirred the embers with a branch. "That's how they are successful, Brigid. You've just said it. The Brothers here have shown faith. By giving away his cow, Brother Ailbe showed faith."

I stared into the fire. Giving away the cow had been my idea. How far was I willing to go in order to help those with whom we fundamentally disagreed?

"Patrick shows his hope, too," Dar added. "He *did* donate the animals." She glanced at me at the mention of his name, but I said nothing. Patrick was something separate, quiet, alone. "The Christians visibly show hope in the future. Do druids do the same?"

"Sometimes, but not often enough. Many give predictions, or follow sacrifices. Are we hopeful?"

"That's why Mel likes you," Dar said. "You have that hope. You share. You empathize. Druids like Maithghean, and Dubhtach do not. Apparently, these Unisech druids do not."

"You show that hope too, my friend. Without your support, we'd have no school at all. I owe you a lot." The embers hissed and glowed. "Do you feel like we are approaching something new? Something we haven't thought of yet?"

"A new path," said Dar. "I see it, but I can't explain it. A blend, yet separate. It's..."

She couldn't explain it and neither could I.

"Before we continue home, may we have a moment to meditate in your chapel?" I asked Brother Ailbe in the morning. "We performed our sunrise ritual outside earlier but we'd also like a few moments with the oak in the chapel."

"Ah, certainly you may," Brother Ailbe agreed, bewildered. I was sure he had not had many druid requests for rituals in their chapel. "Perhaps we may all join in silent prayer together."

Mel, drank his early morning wine, sat in a pew and recited his Latin prayers aloud. Brother Ailbe and Brother Declan joined him. The nuns filled in the benches behind them. Dar and I acknowledged the light of a new day with up-raised arms. Then we knelt down at the front altar, surrounded by oak and rowan. Energy soared through us. We joined hands and grasped an oak branch with our free hands. We made our circuit connect between earth, tree, and ourselves.

What about us? A cry came as I reached into the earth for power. *You do your work in a church, and we will be forgotten.* Dagda and Macha, all of the Danann, called to me. Was I betraying the Ancient Ones, like Patrick did? Yet, he only made the promises of a captive shepherd, unable or unwilling to remember his past. *I'm not forgetting you,* I replied to them silently. *We need their help. It's the only way. All students of Cill Dara will remember your name.*

Power flowed through me, and I touched the base of the old oak altar for grounding. The wood was aged, and I felt a sense of wisdom seep from it as Mel spoke his Latin words.

"Bishop," the brothers whispered, interrupting him.

"Mel," said Mariah.

Mel ignored the monks and nuns as well and continued with his spoken prayers. I was deep in meditation, flowing energy into the earth, to the Danann. *Take my strength,* I told them. *Understand the choices I've made.*

Irritated, I opened my eyes when Mel placed his hands on my head, an obviously rude interruption. I looked into the beaming red-faced Bishop Mel. "You're a Christian now, Brigid, officially the true abbess of Cill Dara."

"What?" I asked. Dar and I still knelt at the altar, my hand on the oak tree. "I took no vows nor made any promises."

"Bishop Mel," Brother Ailbe interrupted again. "You said the wrong vows. You didn't make her a Christian, and it didn't look to me like she was asking to be one. You ordained her as a Bishop."

Bishop? How could he have ordained me a bishop? Mel was drunk on wine and didn't even know what he was doing. Brother Declan, however, was more concerned with the altar. He pointed past me with wide eyes. "Look at what she's done."

On the thick branch that I had grasped, new green growth sprouted. Green shoots unfolded.

Dar still held her side of the branch and nothing sprouted there. She, for once, looked as amazed as the others. The Danann gifts I had been striving for began their reclamation. An uncontrolled flow of energy from the earth had passed through me as I meditated. Energy from old gods.

Loud voices filled the previously quiet chapel. Brother Ailbe argued with Mel and demanded he retract the ceremony that made me a bishop. Mel maintained that a binding promise to God was made, whether I was cognizant of it or not. God decreed it, so and who was he to question the will of the Lord?

"Look at the miracles!" he cried to Brother Ailbe. "A live plant grows beneath her hands! I will not deny God the miracle."

Dar whispered to me in the midst of the milieu. "This could be to your advantage, Brigid. With Maithghean invoking your slave status, you are still in danger when you leave Cill Dara. You need something to call your own. A status with rights and power, for your own protection."

"We're not Christian! 'm not a nun or abbess or bishop, nor do I want to be." She had a point about my precarious slave status. Leaving Cill Dara without Bishop Mel or a guard at my side was dangerous. According to strict interpretation of Brehon law, I was a slave. If my father did indeed sell me to Maithghean, he had every right under Irish law to claim me when I was outside of Cill Dara's gates.

"It could also be a new path for the druids, a new path for our people. This is what came to me just now, as we prayed. We cannot do this on our own. Not anymore." She took my hands, her blue eyes fervent. "Fight for yourself, before these ignorant men convince Mel otherwise."

"It doesn't even make sense."

"None of it does. Think of the advantages. You would have access to all the people of our land. You would have your freedom. Money and finances would no longer be a problem. Division between them and us no longer works. Look at our school. Unintentionally, our partnership with them works. We can't cling to our separate sides any longer."

"Should we become more involved with the Church. More involved than we already are? More involved than shared land, schools, and charities?"

"Christianity is a presence in Éire, and we can't defeat it," said Dar. "We are merging with it, just as you practice to merge with stone. That is the path."

"No..." I echoed. I wanted to defeat it. I wanted it gone because it was a threat to the old ways, to the ancient ones, the Danann, forever underground. The only threat was ourselves. Our own corruption, our own ineptitude. "We must survive. What will become of the Ancient Ones, the druids, the very gods and goddesses of this land?"

"If you accept what Mel has given you," said Dar, "you will always be there to correct the wrongs. The priests will not be able to twist words. You will make them tell our stories true.You would even have power over Patrick."

"Patrick." His name brought me back to the present. If I accepted this haphazard position, I would, at some point, have contact with him.

"He's not a bishop," continued Dar. "He came to Éire, on his own and he has yet to be formally consecrated. The church administration is not happy with him." I questioned how my friend knew so much about the man I considered my secret. "Mel told me," she said. "I asked about Patrick as we traveled."

It was true. Patrick came to Éire as a renegade. The Church still, years later, refused to grant him an official post; Mel had told me the same in one of his wine-soaked conversations. Yet, he converted more Irish than anyone had before in Éire. He should be a bishop now, and I just gained the title by a drunken man's mistake.

"Please, Brigid, explain to him again that you didn't intend to take any vows," Brother Ailbe pleaded, interrupting Mel's speech about God's will and the oak tree miracles.

"I'm sorry?" I asked innocently, as Brother Ailbe's eyes widened. "Of course I did. I accept the position as Bishop of Cill Dara."

CHAPTER 18

Brigid

C onleth, the priest Bishop Mel promised, joined Cill Dara at the beginning of summer to oversee the Christian community. He moved his belongings into the monks' quarters and hurriedly joined me to review the organization for the nuns. I welcomed the stocky blond man, but he didn't return my overtures of friendship. Our first meeting was tinged with acrimony.

"I accepted this post from Mel because I believe it is God's will that I be here," Conleth said. "I thought, wrongly, I would be serving alongside another Christian."

"You may think what you wish about my management. Bishop Mel and I have an arrangement so that both schools succeed."

"Using church funds," he retorted.

"The church funds are used only for building materials and food, which we all share. Druids need little materials, but for the land and the sky and sun above us."

"You're not a Christian," he charged. "Yet you call yourself a bishop."

I stepped back. Conleth didn't know me. "Mel calls me a bishop. Don't hold me responsible for his mistakes. There are a few others who are foolish enough to believe the rumors: messengers, visitors." I held up my hands in feigned helplessness. "Don't blame me for what others choose to see."

"It's still a deception. This is church land, a community built by Christians."

"The school of the Sacred Oak was here before the Christians. Mel begged me to share the land with him. Begged," I added to make my point. "Does the Church now own it? Yes, but the druids were here first."

He was finally silent for a moment. "Cill Dara is not what I expected," he said.

I didn't tell him the other reason why I stayed - slavery. Maithghean's threats could be made real if I ever set foot off this land alone. I needed the title of bishop to save me. "I promised Mel I would help in any way I could. Mariah refused the offer. No nuns would take this job, nor would you, apparently." He started to interrupt, but I continued. "I will handle the administrative needs for Cill Dara on the women's side, ordering supplies, orienting new students, scheduling classes, and greeting officials who may visit. Mariah was offered the position," I repeated. If Conleth didn't like this situation, he could take it up with her. "She wanted more time to study illumination and the healing arts. I will not set foot in your chapel, if that is what you prefer."

Dar and I taught druids while a growing number of Christians joined the monastery. Though each side had their own course of studies, several classes and apprenticeships were shared. Healing, metalwork, music, nuns and druids attended together. As we spoke, Catha, our budding bard, and one of the Christians nuns walked past, discussing Biblical genealogies as compared to Irish ones. Conleth's lips upturned at the corners, a slight movement which dropped when he saw me watching him.

Conleth kept to himself during his first weeks at Cill Dara. I guessed he was, by nature, a warm and friendly man, but he distrusted the druid presence. He got along well with the monks and always had a smile on his face in their presence. He witnessed examples of how Cill Dara blended together. Several nuns attended our rituals as observers, while a few druids took an avid interest in the arts of illumination. They'd begun to learn a written alphabet, but were still required to memorize and recite their histories. Conleth couldn't help but see the exceptionality of our dual institution. I, too, had to admit it worked better than I ever imagined. We heard occasional protest from túaths that the druid acolytes here were not being taught in the traditional way.

However, the far away druids did not know, or see, my efforts at reviving the Danann talents of blending with an element. Only Dar, Catha, and myself worked on Danann meditation. We each claimed an element: I, to stone, Dar to water, Catha to earth. So far, I was the only one to achieve even a hint of merging. My hand, occasionally, would sink and I could watch the weird blur of flesh and stone. It took hours of concentration and focus. These were things, I knew, Danann children could learn before their tenth year. Lugh helped me with the flame, but even he no longer had the energy to give to me anymore. *You have to find your old gifts, Brigid..*

The straw and thatch chapel built by Mel's original monks was in disrepair. Instead of rebuilding the thatch, Conleth announced their next church would be made of stone. "Like Peter on the rock," he'd said. He and his monks cleared the ground - right next to the courtyard and the flame.

"We're on our side of the property," Conleth said before I could ask why he wanted his chapel so close to the perpetual flame.

"You're very close to the druids. Are you sure some magic won't sneak over?" I teased him, trying to get a smile to show on his reserved face. It worked.

"Are you worried your druids might turn Christian?" he teased back. I laughed but wondered at the truth of his question.

Secretly, I was fascinated. A building of stone. I'd never seen such a thing. They removed stones from the soil, so their church would have the smoothest floor. They saved those stones for the church walls.

One day, I watched without Mariah. The monks lifted and pushed and hauled. Another monk wielded a mallet to chip away at the sharp corners of stones.

While Conleth worked, a heavy rock rolled back and crushed his hand as he dug, leaving him with broken fingers and a deep gash. He groaned in pain.

"I need Mariah." Conleth said as I rushed to his side to examine his hand.

"Mariah is in Dun Ailenn, assisting with a birth."

Conleth's face contorted, whether in pain from his injury or the fact he would have to be treated by a druid, I didn't know. His face flushed against his fair hair, as he leaned on the partially built wall of the church.

"Not here," I insisted. "You should be treated in the healing lodge where I have supplies."

Cautiously, he staggered to his feet and leaned on one of his young monks for support as we walked to the lodge. "I'd prefer to wait for Mariah."

"I won't harm you," I said. "Mariah will be away for hours." It was ridiculous that he even questioned my professionalism. We made it to the lodge, and Conleth slumped on the bench. I feared he might faint, but he cringed when I reached for his injured hand.

"Everything Mariah learned was from me," I said sharply. He nodded and closed his eyes. Did he expect that I would whisper magic spells over his injury? I might. A few wouldn't hurt. He seemed surprised when I washed his wounds with water and covered the cuts with a garlic and honey paste. Finally, I set his two first fingers with splints, working quickly as the man winced in pain.

"Here, drink this," I handed him a steaming cup.

Conleth drew back. "I don't want any potions."

"It's willow bark," I snapped, exasperated. "You're Irish. Why do you fear a druid healer?" He was undoubtedly raised in a village with druids and a competent healer.

"My mother turned to Christ after my father died in battle, when I was a young boy. We joined one of the coastal communities. We had healers, of course, but they were Christian."

"You must have known druids who could heal at some point. Where you grew up doesn't explain your distrust."

Conleth lifted his splinted hand and winced. The willow bark tea would help ease the pain, but he'd need to drink the first cup completely.

"My father died at the hands of a druid," he said finally. "A sword destroyed his innards during battle, and the supposed druid healer let him die."

I flinched at the pain his father must have felt. Death was a grateful escape.

"My mother never trusted them again," he continued. "The call of Christ was strong, so we left."

"Battle wounds such as those are difficult, if not impossible, to heal. Your father couldn't have survived no matter if his healer was druid or Christian."

He sipped his tea, holding the cup in his good hand. A beam of light filtered into the room, shining on the multi-colored blankets of wool and the shelves of plants and herbs that decorated the healing lodge. Conleth studied the space.

"Perhaps," Conleth said finally. He glanced at me shyly. "Thank you, Brigid, for helping me."

CHAPTER 19

Brigid

I sank into the stone. My energy blended. My pulse, my heartbeat, centered into the rock. I delved deeper and became one with the quartz within, the crystalline center of the stone. The spark was there, the beginning of fire that upheld the flame, and I sank into it. I rejoiced in the absolute silence surrounding me.

"Brigid." The worried voice shocked me out of the stone. I awoke the forest behind Cill Dara. Dar knelt by my side. Her face was white with fear. "I saw you. You were with the rock. Part of it. As if you'd melted right into it."

I lay on my back, on top of the boulder where I worked, exhausted. Dar and Catha both peered over me, worried. "I'm tired," I said. "I might have to wait awhile before walking back to the school."

"How did you do it?" asked Catha. "Every time I feel like I'm getting close, something pushes me away."

"It's the same for me," said Dar. "I begin to feel liquid, like I'm part of the stone." My throat and mouth were as dry as stone. I could tell them how I accomplished it. I still retained some small piece of the Danann within me, enough to accomplish this task even when Lugh could no longer help. It felt as if all the strength left my body. I was limp, a wet rag. I tried to speak again, but then shook my head. If I could do this, then Dar and Catha would believe they could, too. They didn't know about my Danann past. Dar, I believe, had an inkling. I couldn't explain to her all of the Danann past without including Patrick...Padraic. Padraic and I shape shifted together. We'd sink into the stone together. We connected on an elemental level, a place beyond soul or spirit. If

I could do this beginning of shape shifting now, then there was a good chance Patrick could, too.

"Brigid, Dar - come quickly!" Dar and I rose from sleep and stumbled through the dark, hurrying outside to the urgent voices of the women.

"Look!" The nuns rushed us to the chapel door.

I was puzzled as to why the nuns dragged us out of bed in the middle of the night.

"The infant," said Mariah. "There, on the steps."

I looked to where she pointed, and there indeed was a tiny baby, wrapped in rough wool. I picked it up swiftly, while the nuns gasped.

"Why didn't you bring the child inside?" I asked. It was strange to think they wouldn't touch the baby and left it lying on the ground. "Mariah, you're a healer. Why would you leave the baby here?"

"We were afraid," said Caitlin, a novice nun.

"Afraid of what?" Dar and I spoke in unison. Christian and druid offered shelter and healing to those in need at Cill Dara, and there should have been no reason to fear an infant.

"Fairies," Caitlin explained. "It's a fairy child, a changeling, left here."

"Well, it can't be a changeling." I checked through the swaddling. "She can't be a changeling," I corrected. The baby coughed, a horrible, deep sound from the tiny body. She burned with fever.

"It's bad luck," said Mariah. "Picking up a fairy baby."

I held the infant close to my chest. I kept my voice low and my rage was spoken through clenched teeth. "If I'm going to continue to train you as a healer, then you will tend to all children, changeling or not. Don't you ever leave a baby exposed like this." Mariah looked to the ground. Well, she should be ashamed, I thought. They believe in fairies and changelings, I thought as the Danann gave my consciousness a quick tug. If everyday folk took the superstition for truth, what hope was there for the Danann to be freed? New beliefs, new superstitions came with Christianity.

"There is no such thing as changelings," Dar reprimanded the group of women, as though she read my thoughts. "Our gods and goddesses disappeared when they were defeated in battle, but they aren't the sprites you believe them to be. Don't ever leave a sick or hurt infant outdoors like this. What is wrong with you?"

She lectured the nuns who should have known better, and reminded them that the Danann had been people endowed with magical gifts, not fairies. I took the feverish infant to the healing lodge. I cooled her down with wet rags and searched through my pharmacy of herbs to find something for her cough. The baby was too young for tea. I would need to make a plaster for her chest and hope it worked. The infant wrenched with hacking coughs and her tiny body convulsed in my arms.

As tiredness overwhelmed me, I wondered why Conleth wasn't awakened with this emergency. The child was left at the church, after all, not on the druid side, near the flame or under the oak.

"What is your name, young one?" I asked her while I worked. She kicked and screamed, gasping for breath in between the coughs. Her entire body turned red with the effort, and her face was as almost as dark as her hair. Panicked, I picked her up, allowing her breath to return.

"Melwyn," I decided. The Welsh-sounding name came to me as I held her. "Melwyn, this will soothe your cough," I spread the plaster, allowing the vapors to penetrate into her lungs. I studied the girl, determined to make her live.

The tension between Conleth and I lessened after he shared the details of his father's death. I understood, even if I didn't agree with his distrust of druids. He began to show his friendlier side. He visited the healing lodge several times a week, ostensibly so I could check on his injury, but I suspected he was taken with the baby, the once-feared changeling, Melwyn.

"How is the child?" He asked as I removed the last of his bandages from his hand. His fingers had set and the gash healed.

"She's thriving." Then a chill swept over me. I had a vision, not an image from the past, which is what I was used to, but a flash to the future. Instead of a fresh scar, I saw Conleth's hand covered in blood. I swayed, dizzy, not used to the seer's vision. "Brigid, what is it?"

"Danger comes to you. See the blood which covers you?" I blinked again and the vision evaporated.

"Blood? What are you saying?" Conleth drew his hand away.

The blood was a foreshadowing. Clairvoyance was Dar's gift, not mine. My head pounded, and I felt the old lightheadedness of a Danann memory return. "I had a premonition of you in harm's way."

Suspicion showed again on his readable face. Conleth distrusted druids. He distrusted anything unclear or unexplainable. "I don't know what it means. I've rarely had visions like that."

He snatched his hand away and studied the red scars across his knuckles. I didn't want to lose his trust, not now. We had reached a working relationship after his initial hostility toward the presence of druids at Cill Dara. He darted his eyes to Melwyn, as though he questioned an infant in my care.

"It's probably nothing," I said. "Just be careful with your hand as you continue building your church. I might have been worried about a future injury."

"That's all?" he asked "I'll be careful not to bash any more stones on my hand." He smiled nervously. He checked on Melwyn, who lay in her basket, cooing.

"I'm sure it is. Be careful lifting rocks." I put away the bandages and salves, as the baby clutched his newly healed index finger in her hand.

"I'm only waiting for the last of her cough to clear up," I said.

"Do you like children?" I asked.

"I had several younger sisters. I had no interest in them then, of course." He let the infant grab his finger again, and she waved his clutched digit in the air. "Someday," he said softly.

"Excuse me?"

"Oh," he looked up and blushed. "I didn't realize I spoke aloud. I just meant that someday, I would like to have a family, children."

The ticking in my mind began. The pulse. The Ancients. A memory... I had not had a new one for years... *Patrick...Padraic...someday.* Then we'll stay here. We will have a farm, raise children...He'd wanted a family...with me...we talked about those things. I now vividly remembered conversations, thoughts, feelings...much more than the purely physical scene that made me run away in confusion years ago.

"Brigid?" Conleth waited for my response as I broke free from my daze.

"I'm sorry," I apologized, embarrassed. "It happens, sometimes...dizziness."

"You're shaking," Conleth led me to the bench and wrapped my cloak around me. I huddled in its warmth, trying to reconcile the images I recalled with the man I knew now as Patrick.

Conleth watched me, his brown eyes shining with concern. He stayed next to me.

"Brigid?"

"I'll be fine, Conleth, really." I touched his hand in appreciation, but I stayed seated, waiting for the lightheadedness to subside. Conleth rummaged through my dried herbs. "What are you doing?"

"I'll make you some tea."

I relaxed, finding his concern comforting. I was glad to know the young monk had a caring soul.

CHAPTER 20

Brigid

Christianity was a fact now in Éire. More people began to follow the new beliefs as they continued to practice our Solstice rituals, Beltane, Samhain. As much as I wanted to argue against the new god, I found I couldn't. Bishop Mel had done nothing but help me. We shared a goal of ending tribalism and slavery. I could only keep my ages-old promise to the Danann, faded in time, between pasts and memories. In the years since Cill Dara's inception, I tried to salvage what I could, to teach my students at Cill Dara what needed to be remembered, and keep what I could of the Túatha de Danann spirits.

The Danann whispered in the cool night air, as the flame wavered in the wind. To what end? The Danann time is past. It is a new world now filled with new beliefs, a small voice whispered inside me as I lay alone in my bed, listening to the soft sound of Dar's rhythmic breathing across the room.

Patrick made promises as well, I thought to myself late into the night. I wanted to make him remember those promises. When he mentioned the Danann, he convoluted their meaning, a strategy that worked. That was the piece that continued to trouble me, even as I accepted the presence of another belief. Is a reminder of old promises the true reason you wish to see him again? So he can combine our names with the stories of his god? Was his warped message better than no message at all? An old anger. I couldn't conjure up any fire with it. The Danann, the Christians. They were all bigger than him, bigger than us. So what? I thought to myself in the darkness. So what?

In the intervening years since the Test of the Ancients, my memories sharpened and focused. I had little control over their emergence and less control over when one of the Danann decided to communicate with me. It must have been like this for Patrick when he was enslaved, not knowing when I would talk to him. I wanted to find him so he could find his memories again, so he could remember Padraic, so he could sink into stone with me. I closed my eyes in the darkness, reliving the memories again. The images came, unbidden, of our flesh meeting. The summer on the mountain was another lifetime ago. I loved him then. I still did.

"The officials of Cill Dara have been invited to Armagh to discuss the goals of the Christian church in Éire." Conleth opened the scrolled piece of vellum, delivered to our gates by a travel-worn monk. Bishop Mel visited with us and listened to the words as Conleth read them aloud. We met in the courtyard, the halfway point between the church and the oak. The flame burned, still bright.

Writing and reading were difficult for me. I learned a few words by studying Mel's neatly written letters but felt I was compromising my vows as a druid. New letters, new words, a new language.

"It is imperative," Conleth continued reading, "that the Irish Church create its own community, independent in its own right. Signed, Patrick, Bishop of Armagh."

A faint cry came from the hollow of my soul. In a brief flash, I saw his eyes, the color of the sea on a clear day.

"Well, he's not a bishop, first of all," said Conleth rather snidely.

Mel waved his hand. "He should be. He's converted more people than I, or any other priest on this island, have."

"Then why isn't he a bishop?" I asked, although I knew the answer. Still, if Mel could ordain me, he should be able to ordain Patrick.

"I can tell what you're thinking Brigid. I can't. I've been warned many times by the Cardinal. He's not to be ordained. He's caused too many problems, starting when he ran off here on his own, without permission. If I ordained him, I'd lose my position here, and you would lose your school."

He took the letter from Conleth. "Patrick is suggesting we cut all ties with the church in Britannia, and, therefore, Rome..." Mel's voice quieted as if the bishops and cardinals overseas could hear him.

Conleth nodded. "I'm not in disagreement. Éire is an island and people all to herself. Britannia and Rome rarely notice our existence unless it is time to pay tithes. It has all of our names on here," Conleth glanced at me. "The word of your misdirected bishop's ordination has spread."

I brightened. Patrick wrote the letter. He had to have written my name and title. As bishop. Did he know it was me, or did he address his letter to an anonymous nun?

Mel wrung his hands. He knew the potential difficulties of our land agreement, particularly if church authorities asked to meet with me. He and Conleth were some of the few who knew my title was in name only. I was a druid. I practiced druid rituals and taught healing to the druids. My college trained young women and men in the druid craft, healing craft. It seemed their druids were in decline as Christians moved into their villages. I sighed, thinking of what I helped to create. I had no right to see the self-proclaimed leader in Armagh. I laughed as Conleth and Mel glanced in my direction. Patrick wasn't a bishop any more than I was, yet he had appointed himself the leader of a new Irish church.

"As interested as I am in this discussion, I can't go," Conleth replied to Mel. "We leave for the south. We promised the new communities there we would visit."

I bit my lip. I should be the one to go. I should see Patrick. I hadn't seen him since the day on the mound...and together we created fire.

"We can send Brother Thomas." Conleth spoke with his usual authoritative-ness.

Mel considered the invitation. "Thomas is coming with us. We can't spare him for Armagh. We do need someone to represent Cill Dara, someone who understands our administrative process and our communiqués with the Ro-man bishops. I'm certain Patrick writes to us particularly for another reason, since we are gaining students from the north, those that ought to be joining his monastery."

I thought of Mariah. She came because Conleth offered her leadership roles. She chose to learn more, to study, and turn any administrative work over to me. Her students and mine now studied healing together. It was unorthodox, but it worked. *I looked for you*...Patrick's voice echoed in my mind as my heart rang hollow. I wanted to see him. Not to discuss church and druid politics, nor the mission given to him by the Túatha de Danann. I wanted to see him for myself, to explain my disappearance.

"I'll go!" I burst out to Mel.

"You can't go!" Conleth bellowed, and his face turned red. "You're a druid!" Mel and I both turned to watch the frustration rise within the young priest.

"I know your numbers as well as you, how many students we have and the cost of housing them," I stated firmly. "I've spoken to visitors here on your behalf." I glared at Conleth, reminding him of the extra tasks I completed for him when he became too busy. "If Patrick wants our support for his independent church, I'll say whatever you wish." I dug my heels into the earth, unwilling to compromise, particularly with Conleth.

"Our support? What do you care? Send Mariah," Conleth insisted to Mel. "Send some class of Christian to meet the most powerful priest in the land." Conleth's theatrics would have been amusing if I didn't want to go so badly.

"As far as Patrick knows, Brigid of Cill Dara is a Christian, a bishop. He did address the letter to her," Mel said.

I shot a smug look in Conleth's direction. Mel walked away from us both, as a parent would ignore his clamoring children. We waited impatiently for his answer, as he paced around the courtyard.

"We cannot spare many here if we go south at the same time," Mel said finally. He sat on the bench and stared contemplatively at the flame. "Shearing is to be done, planting as well. Those chores are left to those not going south with us."

"Then we will put off the mission," Conleth argued. "It can wait a few more weeks. You and I will go to Armagh ourselves."

"We can't wait, Conleth. We have already promised the southern communities we would arrive a week after Beltane. Building must be completed before the autumn rains begin." Conleth sighed in annoyance. He knew Mel was right. They had delayed this particular trip more than once.

"Please, Mel," Conleth's voice dropped to a whisper. "There must be somebody else who can represent Cill Dara at this meeting." There wasn't. Novice monks and nuns shouldn't know the details of this letter, which was basically treason against the church.

I rolled my eyes, irritated at Conleth's vehement protests. I stepped between the two men. "Conleth, as far as the rest of Éire knows, I'm a Christian bishop ordained by Mel. I'm sorry if you dislike it, but there is nothing to be done." I took a deep breath, saving my final warning. "If you would like to announce my status to the Christian world, feel free. I shall be happy to bid you farewell when your church forces you to leave this land since you've known about the druid school all along." His eyes left mine and met Mel's.

"She's right," Mel agreed. "Conleth, if you choose to make a fuss about this, it could cost you the monastery. The Church does not know how intricately we co-exist with the druid community here."

"The church paid for the land," Conleth argued. "How could the bishops in Britannia not know?"

Mel reddened and cleared his throat. "I may have mentioned several successful conversions. There had been a few. Including Brigid." Sheepishly, Mel turned to me. "Brigid," he began as Conleth's fists clenched in anger. "You will travel to Armagh for us. Find out what plan Patrick has. Listen to him and report to us. Don't give him an answer. Don't enter into any agreements. And for heaven's sake, don't sign your newly-learned signature on anything. We'll discuss whether or not we agree with Patrick's revolutionary ideas when we all get back from our travels."

Conleth sat on the bench heavily, cradling his head in his hands. I smiled. The first part of my battle was won.

CHAPTER 21

Brigid

My breath caught as I stood in the doorway of Patrick's roundhouse, studying the man I'd waited so long to see.

His abode followed the ascetic model of isolated Christians that dotted the coastline: plain, simple as an offering to God. The willow-bough ceiling was permeated with smoke from the smoldering hearth.

Patrick sat at a vellum-strewn desk, reading. His eyes strained upon the written words. Lines encircled his eyes as evidence of this habit, and white streaked his black hair. His brown robe, worn thin, had patches sewn on the elbows that were more pronounced as he held a document closer to the candlelight. There was no evidence of an illustrious priest or a powerful self-proclaimed bishop. Only an older outline of the boy I once knew.

"Patrick."

His head sprang up, startled at my presence. He swallowed hard. "Who let you in?"

I removed my rain-spattered cloak. "We have a meeting."

"You? You're the Bishop of Cill Dara?" His face contorted into an agonized frown, and his right hand clenched the vellum that he had been reading. "You're *that* Brigid? How?"

I nodded slowly and felt an ache deep within. We had not met since the day he preached. Neither of us moved. I saw him as the young man who was forced to be an isolated shepherd. I saw farther, into the past, the man who fought to save the Danann even when they had cast him out, the man who had been my best friend, my partner, my anam cara. He, too, seemed lost, perhaps wondering if this was a dream. I walked toward him, hugging my cloak to my chest.

"Patrick," I reached across his desk to touch his hand. He snatched it away as if it was burned.

"I'm a man of God." His voice cracked and his blue eyes blazed. "You are...I don't know who you are. Not anymore."

"A lot has happened. I don't know how to explain it all." I suddenly realized I was disheveled and travel-worn. A monk tended to the mule upon my arrival, placing Clover in the monastery barn. He offered to show me to the guest house, but I refused, eager to see Patrick. Self-conscious, I brushed a stray oak leaf off my skirt, smoothing the dark blue wool, a dark robe that passed for either a druid or a nun. I hadn't taken the time to braid my hair, and copper waves flowed freely down my back.

The candlelight flickered and shadows alternated between us. His mouth worked as though he tried to speak, to find his voice.

"I came as you requested," I began for him. "Conleth sends his regrets, but he and Bishop Mel already made mission plans."

He stepped away from his desk, and his head touched the willow bough ceiling. "You left me," he began as if retelling a story to a small child, "Long ago, when I was alone in the west, and then no so long ago, when I preached to a village. What am I supposed to do?"

Silence. I couldn't explain how my anger overwhelmed me. I behaved miserably, governed by an uncontrollable reaction when I saw him preach. I needed to explain to him about the kidnapping.

Patrick heaved a huge sigh and tried to stifle a sob. A horrible mass of guilt weighed down upon me. Patrick failed me. Those words I'd repeated to myself often. I hadn't admitted to myself that, just as equally, I'd failed him.

"What happened to you, Brigid? Please tell me so I can make some sense of this. Explain to me the dreams. You came to me in dreams...I know your voice...and your touch."

Of course he knew. His memories as dreams. This is what I tried to teach him, our past together, our lives as the Ancient Ones. How could I explain time and space spiraling in on itself? How could I explain the world of spirits and reincarnation to a man who didn't believe?

"I can't change the past," I fumbled for words. "I couldn't come back to you when I went to see Dathi. Maithghean and the Fotharit druids took me. Kidnapped me. Raven kept Dathi in the fort. I tried to find you later but you had escaped." I wiped a tear from my cheek and continued, determined to account for my actions. "That day when you preached. I didn't understand what happened to me. The anger flowed through me. My anger, yes. But the past, the other Brigid, too."

He seized my shoulders, his hands as hot as the smoldering presence of embers, which glowed in the far recesses of the room. "Who are you? What are you?"

"I'm Brigid. I always have been," I whispered, willing him to remember all that I had told him. In the stillness, we held a conversation with our eyes. *I never stopped loving you.* "It's difficult to explain. I didn't know everything when I heard your sermon. Memories come to me every day. You remember when that happened in Foclut Forest?"

"When I preached," he seemed to want to ignore what happened that summer. "You knew me. You knew enough to chastise me in front of my followers."

"I knew you promised to help me save the Túatha de Danann."

He shook his head, perplexed. "I never made those promises. You and Dathi wanted me to. But I never agreed."

"We worked on those memories together. Don't you remember? *Padraic?*"

"No. You've tried to make me remember that name...before..."

"You almost did. When you were a shepherd, we worked very hard at remembering our past together."

"I was a slave. I'd been kidnapped, beaten. All sorts of insane thoughts went through my head during that time."

I tried again. He'd remembered before.. "I was once of the Túatha de Danann. We both were. They are still part of me, part of my past, although very long ago."

"You came to me as a woman, a druid helping Dathi. You were not of the Danann. Not a goddess. You were human. You looked as you do now."

Heat rose in my face, recalling the passion we shared. "That summer..." my voice quivered. "I only started to remember. I didn't understand. But now I've had years of visions. Memories. Do you know what it is like to see something, suddenly, that you didn't know existed?"

He spoke wryly. "You."

We both smiled together and waited in the silence. He was in front of me, after all these years. Tall, lanky. His blue eyes were still piercing. I wanted to reach for him again, but each time I did, he pulled away.

"I dreamt of you when I was a child in Fotharit." I continued quietly, finally. "I didn't know who you were. You were always there to help me and save me from those who wanted to destroy me." He had appeared to me for years, and I didn't know. What I wanted for my whole life, and beyond, was here. The last of the dying embers hissed as they fell into ash. The room turned dark, save for the lit candle on his desk.

I touched his face and let my fingers trace his jaw line. I inhaled his scent. Peat and rain were part of him. He carried with him the open fields where he had spent so many lonely years. My fingers touched the rough growth of his beard and his smooth skin underneath.

He closed his eyes, giving in. "Brigid." He stroked my cheek with a single fingertip. "Do you remember what we were to each other?"

"I remember."

We sighed together, voices quiet, touching, fingertips to hand to face. It was as if the place where we now stood didn't matter, as if no time had passed. With stunning clarity, I remembered the softness of his mouth.

"I've wanted to see you for so long, not in dreams. I heard your voice when I was in Gaul. You said I must return here," he whispered.

My fingertips continued their journey along his features, his along mine. "I knew you were chosen for holy work here in Éire."

His touch faltered, and he rested his hand on my shoulder. I didn't move, willing his hand to stay. If he let go completely, all would be lost.

"You knew this?" His other hand was tangled in my hair. Every touch was magic, making the lines of energy flow through both of our bodies. He might not have remembered his past, but his soul did. His body did. We connected, drawn toward each other. "You knew I was meant for the priesthood?" He pulled his hand free, and the heat began to dissipate into a chill down my spine. The spell was broken.

Holy work. I meant holy *druid* work. Danann work. That was not what he heard.

"All that I taught you and what we practiced. I told you of Éire and her gods and goddesses." Then something else, someone else, the Danann past from below rose into me. *Don't forget who I am.*

He pushed me away. "Yet, here I am Brigid. You abandoned me and I turned to this. You and your gods didn't help me. The Tuatha dé Danann didn't help me. They didn't come for me when I was enslaved. They didn't help me escape to the harbor, to row on ships, for the Germani until they finally brought me to Britannia. The Danann, these so-called Ancient Ones, and you, left me completely alone. The only one to help me was God. My god. Not yours."

I grappled for words, unable to comprehend that the moment that had drawn us together was now gone. "I came to you in Foclut Forest to help you. To teach you about the Ancient Ones because you are connected to them. To us. We needed your help."

"Oh, that's right. You were there to teach me about some long-forgotten past. Was our night together also *instructional*?" His voice was raw and harsh as he strode across the confines of his roundhouse.

"We weren't supposed to fall in love," I was defensive against his sharp tone. He was supposed to remember our past, *that* love. The one before. That love should have been solid. Unchanged. We were to work together and bring the Ancient Ones back to the land. Continue work we began lifetimes before.

"I didn't think my love was one-sided." His eyes grew steely across the room, daring me to contradict.

"That's not what I meant. We didn't have to fall in love, not again, not as something new. We were already together, a solid partnership. Or, we should have been."

"Now," his laugh was hollow, "I've entered the priesthood and you, a nunnery, or monastery, or whatever Cill Dara is, and you are a bishop. Ironic?" He raised his brow. "Despite our decidedly different paths, we are still on the same one, aren't we?"

I smiled weakly, gathering his implications. We took separate roads, yet here we were. Again.

"You aren't a Christian, are you?" he asked, more of a statement than a question. "Have you fooled all of Éire into thinking you are an abbess of a nunnery?"

"I'm a druid of Cill Dara," I said. "Conleth and I teach students of both beliefs. I've not intentionally tried to fool anyone."

"The title of Bishop?" He left the question hanging. He wanted to be bishop, a post refused to him by church authority in Britannia. My title by mistake ought to have been his.

"It is a rumor, Patrick. Mel's drunken mistake. I don't think it counts. It's a rumor many people don't question, but I can't help that."

"So, you threw your anger at me for not teaching about the Danann in the way you wanted," he said. "Now you live side by side with the Church? I'm not sure I'm the one who is the hypocrite here, Brigid."

I burned with anger. "I had to side with them. I had no choice. My father and Maithghean threatened - never mind." I couldn't tell him. Not when he wanted what I had. The title of Bishop.

"The same threats?" His voice softened.

Suddenly, I feared my school was in jeopardy because of the illusion I allowed to continue. Patrick could take it away from me, from Conleth, from Mel. That sort of trickery could work in his favor. He could get the title he wanted so badly. "Patrick, please don't tell the leadership about this. Bishop Mel is a good man, and the arrangement works for us all, even the Church. They've gained more converts from the druid presence. People joined with the druids and ended up with the Christians. The whole thing really works in your favor, not mine." I let words carelessly spill.

He ran his hands through his hair and walked to a basin standing in the corner.

"Which leadership are you referring to? Britannia? Rome?" His smile waned as he paced to the far edge of the room. "I invited you here, or someone from the Christian school of Cill Dara, to discuss an independent church for this island. We can report directly to Rome, and not have to report anything to Britannia. We could skip the British Isles all together."

His plan was dangerous. To separate Éire from Britannia. To make the Irish church its own. I admired him even more for his strength and determination, his belief...turned opposite of what I wanted, of where I planned. *What of the Danann? What of us?*

Patrick turned toward me and his eyes met mine, as though he heard my thoughts.

What of us? He spoke to me silently, as he used to, as Padraic used to. *Even if all you say is true, does it matter now? A millennia too late, are we not?*

Then Patrick turned away. He splashed his face with water from the basin, breaking our communication. He stood with his back to me. I waited, unsure of my next move. Quietly, I approached him.

"You aren't...we aren't..." I began boldly. "We could still be together," I whispered in a rush.

He sighed, looking out his small rough-hewed window etched out of the stone. "I know there are priests here, in Britannia, and on the continent, who have wives, children. My grandfather did. Bishop Mel does."

I hadn't known about Mel's family. He'd never mentioned them, and I had never bothered to ask. My heart leapt with hope. I placed my hand on his shoulder and felt the magic of energy course between my body and his. He stepped aside; my fingers clutched at empty air.

"I made private vows to God that I wouldn't marry. I could, if I wanted to, but I promised when I took on the role of bishop here since there was no one else to do it." His voice was tight and controlled. He traded marriage for his long sought-after title, yet to be officially conferred. "My love, my only love now, is for God, and for the people on this island."

Patrick faced me, his composure regained. The light left his eyes. "Now, Bishop of Cill Dara," he strode to his desk, motioning me to take a seat on the proffered bench. "Tell me what your colleagues instructed you to say."

I sat before him wordlessly, unwilling to believe our love was gone.

CHAPTER 22
Brigid and Patrick

C lover plodded south, as I wallowed in selfish, inconsolable sadness, stung with the pain of rejection. I refused the Armagh monks' offer of shelter for another night and instead stayed in guest lodges along the way. I wanted to return to Cill Dara as soon as I could. It was hopeless. He didn't want our past, or me. I reviewed the conversation with Patrick a million times as I traveled, punishing myself by imagining what I should have done or said differently.

The bog land gave way to gentle hills. I sighed with exhausted relief at the familiar landscape. I skirted around Fotharit and kept to the back forest paths. Even with the title of bishop and recognition of Cill Dara, I didn't trust what Maithghean might do.

The road split in a Y, leading to Cill Dara or Dun Ailenn. Clover shied at the crossroad, refusing to turn as he should.

"Clover, what's the matter?" The mule didn't stand still to chew on the clover patch as he usually did. Instead, he pawed at the ground and brayed. Shouts and screams penetrated my haze of fatigue and I woke from the daze I'd been in. The distant noise broke my contemplation of Patrick. Battle. I knew the sound from my childhood. Warriors beat their shields and bards beat their drums. Women keened as their men were slain, heads dismembered, and bodies left to dry in their own blood.

I snapped Clover with the reins, and, out of fear, he refused to budge. The battlefield on the horizon was wide, encompassing the entire stretch of land between the two roads. Dun Ailenn cattle grazed here. A cattle raid on Dun Ailenn.

As I reached the next hill, I saw a contingent of warriors who strayed far from the battlefield. I tried to go around the fighting, blending into the tall trees of the landscape. Every few steps, I stumbled into another plain of battle. I tried to goad the mule to avoid the fighters, but that path would take me farther away from Cill Dara.

"Damn you, mule, go!" Clover stood stubbornly still. I jumped out and ran away. Instead, I found another band of warriors as they fought along the far border of the forest. The crash of iron and bronze reverberated in the distance, shields and swords striking on one another. Please don't let them kill me, I pleaded to whatever gods or goddesses would listen. I double checked that my copper dagger was tied to my waist.

I should try to blend with the elements, I thought. I know how to do this now. Dar had seen me sink into stone. I could go into the grass. Into the earth. But I couldn't stop and focus. Now was not the time to stop running.

A tall warrior neared me and I saw his ragged kilt and shield. Uí Neill men. They had come from the north to raid Dun Ailenn. I was so close. I could see Cill Dara in the distance. It had yet to be touched by the fighting.

Even in the heat of battle, the Uí Neíll warrior noticed me on the wooded periphery. He scanned the forest for any more enemies. Finding none, he marched toward me. His bare-chest heaved with excitement from his recent kill. Killing me was not what he had in mind. I saw what his torn kilt exposed.

I needed stillness to work druid magic, to access my Danann powers. I needed a calm mind to use the words of protection. Instead, I tightened my hand around the hidden dagger at my belt and bolted into another run.

The warrior lunged and grabbed a handful of my skirt. My head hit the earth so hard I saw stars. I struggled beneath him as he straddled me and pinned me face down into the damp forest earth. I twisted with my dagger, trying to jab at him wherever I could. He grabbed my arm like it was kindling and squeezed my wrist until I dropped the knife. His heavy panting warmed my neck, and his long mustache scratched my face.

"No!" I screamed aloud to every ancient power that I knew. *Macha, Eiru, Dagda...Padraic, help me!*

Patrick slept poorly. Troubled by dreams of Brigid, he left his pallet and returned to his desk in a stupor. He had given the worst homily of his career a few hours earlier, overcome by exhaustion and a sense of unreality. Brigid had been here, in his lodge. She refused to stay and insisted on returning to Cill Dara. He recalled the pained look on her face when he told her of his personal vows. One can't break a promise to God, not for a woman who had deserted him long before.

His hand trembled. It was her...it was her face, her hair, her scent. The smell of clover was unmistakable. He laughed to himself, bringing to mind the name of her mule. Clover. A beautiful name given to such a stupid animal.

The young woman who recently left Armagh had been with him by the campfire years ago. They'd made love. She hadn't wanted to leave. She said she struggled against them, those who took her away. Yet, here she was again, in his home, at his blind invitation, to discuss church business with authority.

He cradled his head in his hands at his desk. Perhaps he would have time for a short nap before the kitchen opened. He and his monks began feeding the local poor once a week, on Sundays after mass. One of Bishop Mel's suggestions. A good one, but it made for a long Sunday.

He closed his eyes and dozed into troubled dreams.

Brigid struggled beneath her attacker. Patrick watched the scene in horror. He was on a dream-like hill, watching the scene.

Stop! He yelled, but to no avail. The ugly brute pawed at her skirts, and Patrick saw the white of her strong leg. His cry of protest was in unison with hers.

Patrick ran, but as in dreams, he moved slowly. God in Heaven, he prayed, to protect this woman. As he ran, lightning struck the ground. Smoke and fire blocked his view.

I must find her. He pushed through the smoke. Then, there he was upon them. God's fire burned the evil man, but he was still alive, moaning in pain.

Patrick raised his shepherd's staff, and with all of his strength, bashed the warrior's skull.

The warrior pushed my long skirt above my hips. I clutched at whatever I could, twigs, leaves, grass, and earth. I gathered all the words of magic that were buried within me, soul beyond soul. I twisted beneath him, trying to turn on my back. I had to look at his eyes if the spell was to work. Beyond druid.

A memory returned. Danann words taught to me by Macha, passed down from mothers, from Danu. A daughter's protection. I reached within and looked for the spark, the fire that raised to my brow. The same fire lit the perpetual flame at Cill Dara. It would work for me now. It had to.

The warrior felt my movement beneath him. He flipped me over and leered into my face as he pushed his battle kilt aside. The sight of his face so near mine made me sick. Focus on the words, focus on the spell, focus on the flame. He clamped his strong warrior hands over my thighs, leaving my hands free. He was hard and rough, like sand against my stomach. I said the words of magic as he pressed himself against me.

I grabbed his face and repeated the secret words. The heat rose from the ground beneath me, flames smoldered beneath my back. I dug my fingernails into his temples and forced his eyes to meet mine as I repeated the ancient phrase. I reached into the earth with all of my being.

Fire burned under me, around me, but I didn't feel it. It was my magic, and it would not work itself against me. The fire did act against him. Flames singed his bare legs and raced to his genitals.

He screamed and rolled off me into another patch of flame. He wrapped his hands around himself, moaning on the ground, but it was too late. I sat up on the charred earth and saw, from the corner of my eye, his skin burned delicate and pink. His eyes met mine. Murder. He would kill me now. He heaved himself up onto his hands and knees. He clawed at the earth and clutched the hem of my skirt again.

Without warning, a stout oak staff seemed to fall from the sky and smashed the warrior's skull. Brain and blood scattered around us. The man fell to the charred ground, never to rise again. Wearily, I sat up on the blackened grasses, prepared to fight off another attacker. Instead, Conleth stood above me, holding the staff, now covered with the warrior's blood.

CHAPTER 23

Brigid

"You can thank Clover for your rescue," Conleth said as he made hot tea in his house behind the chapel. "Your stubborn mule wandered into the courtyard with an empty wagon and a trail of blood. We knew you had been caught in the raid." Dar and Conleth followed Clover's backwards tracks but ended up mired in the battlefield as druids sang songs for the dead.

"It looks like Clover took the most direct route home, through the fighting warriors and bawling cows. I can't imagine what the fighting men thought when this dumb beast ran through." When they reached a dead end, Dar went toward Dun Ailenn. If anyone could, her father would be able to help. Conleth ran to the forest when he saw the smoke and fire.

He handed me the hot mug of chamomile tea, which I held close, glad for something solid and safe. My hands shook.

"For some reason, I thought you would be near fire." His smile waned. Conleth's brow grew tight and his brown eyes vacant. "I killed a man," he whispered.

My heart went out to him. One of the greatest crimes was murder, for both druid and Christian. It wasn't murder. It was a battle. I touched him with a trembling hand. He shook and trembled too. Unlike Patrick, Conleth did not pull away. "You saved me," I said. "You had to do it, to save me."

He lifted his hands, covered in dried blood. My sight doubled and refocused with the recognition of premonition. It seemed like my vision from when he had broken his hand while building the chapel. I looked again. No, his hands were different. Reality did not match the past vision.

"I don't know that I had to save you, Brigid. You seemed to be doing a fine job on your own. That man was terribly burned."

"Then why did you do it? Why did you run all that way with a staff in your hand? How did you know?"

He shrugged. "Dar had her small knife with her, and a pocketful of poisons, I believe. I grabbed the first thing I came across: it could have been a shovel or hoe or a wagon wheel. I took the oak walking stick from where it lay in the forest."

He had not answered my question. I waited, sipping the tea, shaken but grateful to be unharmed. I studied his hands again. The premonition, I thought. I had a vision of Conleth's blood covered hands. This must be the vision come to pass. I would have to ask Dar if visions had to match up exactly.

"I felt like I had to do it," Conleth said. "It was as if something possessed me. I knew where you were. I saw the scene in my head before I arrived." He crossed himself, mystified by the forces that led him to his actions. "As I raised the staff, I knew it was not me," he continued, trancelike. "I saw the man was badly burned and you were uninjured. If it were up to me, up to my own devices, I would have taken you home and left it at that. Brigid, someone else moved my arm. I didn't raise the staff above my head. Something else swung it downward, with such anger, such force. I was enraged that this man would try to violate you. Brigid, in the name of God and all I hold holy, the anger was not mine."

I stayed protected in Conleth's room for as long as I could. The rest of Cill Dara was filled with refugees from the cattle raid, which was the reason he brought me to his quarters. Since the rise of Christianity, the defeated tribes were no longer amenable to slaves gained through kidnapping prisoners of war, as was due course after a battle. They came here instead, because the church would protect those who entered. I certainly had my collection of arguments with the church, and with Patrick, but I welcomed their forthright desire to end bondage in Éire. Slavery should be a relic of the past. I wondered if I'd feel the same if I weren't living under its threat. I supported other things from the past, including the Danann. A fleeing family, along with baby Melwyn, occupied the roundhouse I shared with Dar, and it was not an ideal place to recuperate. Still, my foot tapped, ready to return to my work. The busier I kept myself, the less I would think of what had happened.

"Does Dar know I'm safe?" I asked.

"I sent Cecilia and Brother Thomas to find her," Conleth said. He sank more deeply into the brown wool of his cowl. He had no experience with the other-world, events gone out of his control. Since I was a child, I had been inhabited by strange dreams, magical ideas, ancient gods and goddesses. Growing up in a druid household prepared me somewhat for the effects of the Test of the Ancients, not the physical effects, but I understood the workings of souls and past lives. The shock Conleth must have felt when he described how another entity forced him to kill the warrior was probably indescribable to him.

I glanced out his small window and saw more refugees stream in through our gates. "Conleth?" He stood next to me, his eyes red rimmed from tears. "Conleth, let's go and help these people. What's done is done. He was a warrior attacking a defenseless woman." Well, I wasn't quite defenseless. "He would have probably died in battle anyway."

Conleth's hands still trembled, and blood remained spattered on his robe. I rummaged through the wooden trunk at the end of his pallet and found an identical brown robe.

"Change. Put this on." He looked at me, uncomprehending. "We will burn the old one," I told him. Fire was the best ritual for cleansing, and he would need a potent ceremony to put this event behind him. He took his robe.

Covered in soot and mud, I could have used a change of clothing too. I glanced around the various backrooms of the chapel where extras supplies were stored, but monks didn't weave skirts for women. Any of the women's things were in the roundhouses, now probably used to clothe those who ran from the Uí Neíll. From the window, I saw another family enter my house across the campus. As much as I wanted to keep busy, I didn't feel like facing a roomful of strangers.

Cecilia passed outside the window as I waited for Conleth. I ran out to her.

"Brigid, where have you been?"

"I just returned from Armagh. Bishop Mel and Conleth asked me to go in their place."

"It's a good thing Conleth was here. He came back early from their mission yesterday. He said he wasn't feeling well."

I'd forgotten Conleth was supposed to be working with a new mission in the south. This made his presence on the battlefield even more confusing. He wouldn't have left Bishop Mel unless he really felt the need to return.

Cecilia explained the refugee situation. "We have tens of families here, Brigid. We had to shut the gates." Her eyes filled with tears. "I hated leaving them out like that. They'll probably be taken captive by the Uí Neill. All those families, the children..."

"What about the people who are here?" I asked. "Is everyone within Cill Dara safe?"

"Our guards stand watch and even the Uí Neill know better than to enter here."

We walked to the kitchen. Food preparation had begun for the hundred or so refugees we housed in our small community. Nuns and druids and tribes women worked side-by-side, preparing soups and meat. Our meager winter stores would be depleted, I thought. We could share what we had, but it would be hard to recover from the loss of food. Mariah glanced up at me from where she worked. "Brigid, what happened to you?"

Several women who helped to cook were from the defeated tribe. I noticed the plaid of their shawls. Their colors matched the warrior who attacked me. "Clover. That mule overturned the wagon. I'm going to change, then I'll be back to help you."

Outside, monks gave extra blankets and bedding to women and small children. The setting sun brought an early chill to the displaced families.

"Do we have extra robes for the children?" I asked Cecilia.

"We gave them the spare ones we had. We have no more."

A few of the tribe's women wore the dark blue wool robes of the druids. The majority of refugees wore torn clothing from the battle and their hasty escape. They had no time to gather their belongings. In search of more clothing, I passed a group of men. They talked about a hunt. They wanted to go beyond the gates and track deer, in an effort to add to our dwindling provisions.

"It is too soon after the battle," I warned them. "You could be taken prisoner if you aren't careful. The Uí Neill are swarming all over that field."

"Who are you?" one disheveled man asked bluntly. "There is not enough food here to feed all of us. We can hunt a deer or two, to help with supplies." The men needed something to do. They needed to feel useful after a lost battle. Some of them clutched at ragged cloaks. Others had no shoes.

"I'm Brigid of Cill Dara," I answered his first question. "I returned from my travels in the middle of this mess." I waved my hand at the human confusion. "We have enough food for another day or two. Give the enemy time to gather their cows and go. If you leave the gates now, you'll surely be captured. If you'd like to help, follow me."

I led the rag tag group of men back to the church, where I had seen trunks of clothing stored. Conleth met us as we entered. He looked refreshed in a new robe, and his hands were scrubbed clean of blood. "Brigid, can I help you and these men?"

"We need clothing for the refugees. Most of them left the fort with what they were wearing, much of that destroyed. The druids have given all of our extra robes and supplies."

"Well, we have very little available," Conleth said.

I looked at him in disbelief. I knew he had trunks of clothing stored behind the chapel. I had just seen them. Why would he lie? Was he still dazed from the incident this afternoon?

I stalked past him and went to the closet where trunks were stacked. I tugged the heavy chest out and opened it. Gleaming white robes appeared, and the men rushed toward it to grab handfuls of the warm, thick wool.

"Wait," Conleth said. "This is not clothing for refugees. They are vestments for priests. They are holy articles."

I spun on my heel and glared at the man who had saved my life. "Look at these men, Conleth. They are wearing rags. So are their wives and children. They left their homes with nothing. Certainly you can spare bits of cloth." I joined the men and lifted an armful of robes to hand out in the courtyard.

A few hours later, priests' white robes decorated the grounds of Cill Dara. The Christian monks and nuns were scandalized at the common use of their vestments.

"Brigid, I'm not sure this is allowed," Mariah said, as small children dragged their skirts across the grass. "It's clothing," I stated. "They are cold and the robes are wool and warm. That's all we have."

"Britannia can't find out. Rome can't find out. Do you know how much trouble we'd be in?"

"What about Patrick? Would this sort of thing anger him?"

Mariah laughed. "No, I don't think so. As a matter of fact, I think he'd agree with you completely."

A hefty warrior walked by carrying his massive shield and his scabbard belted nicely around his priest robe. I smiled, and Mariah couldn't help but laugh.

Cill Dara teemed with refugees, and we were all busy with the overwhelming tasks of feeding and clothing our extra guests. The frightened families stayed at Cill Dara until the Uí Neill left the territory. The raiders took cattle and whatever slaves they could find. We promised the first newborn calf from Cill Dara to Dun Ailenn so they could begin to recoup.

"I was more terrified of being kidnapped than of being raped," I reluctantly told Dar after she pressed me to speak about the assault. Alone in our shared home for the first time in a week, we carded wool with wooden-handled brushes. The repetitive motion of brush against brush soothed me. "What if he had taken me out of this territory? What if Maithghean found out? It wouldn't matter if I claimed to be a bishop. Any Brehon could make me a servant, at least as far as they are concerned."

"You shouldn't have traveled there alone. Why did you go to Armagh by yourself, with no guards? That seems foolish, Brigid. I thought Mel sent monks with you."

My face burned at her scolding. She was right. I had relied on the Bishop's title to protect me. I had sent the monks away. I wanted no one from Cill Dara to witness my meeting with Patrick. "I knew if I could just ground myself enough, magic would take care of one horrible man." I shuddered, remembering the warrior's vice-like grip.

"Your magic came very close to not working," she said. "You were lucky Conleth was there to help."

"Well, the magic did work," I said irritably. I knew how close it came. That man's flesh had been on my stomach and thigh. "I made it home."

"Only because I heard you. I felt your distress." She set the cleaned wool in her basket and picked up another tangled handful. "A seer's luck, I suppose."

"I think Conleth is having a harder time recovering than I am."

"He felt it too, you know. We both heard the raid begin and knew we had to find you."

"He doesn't understand any of this." We were both worried about the quiet priest. He seemed more withdrawn than usual, assisting with the kitchen then returning to the rectory as soon as the meal ended.

"He still dwells on how he could have killed a man, even in the thrust of battle, even a man who attacked a defenseless woman," Dar said.

"I wasn't defenseless." Even though I had used the term myself, it began to irritate me. "I called on the fire and it came. The man burned. I don't know what Conleth saw."

"The cattle raid isn't what bothers you," she said. "What is it?"

I had been in shock from the warrior's near-rape, shaken, but I would recover. Patrick and his rejection weighed me down even more. I tortured myself and reviewed our conversation over and over again. I wished I had the memories I now possessed years ago, when I saw him as he preached. Things would have been so different. I let my mind wander. If I had the memories earlier, if I allowed him to come with me instead of leaving him alone in the pasture, if I left Fotharit a day later I would have seen him when he visited. If.

I slowed my brush strokes on the wool. "Before he became a priest. He'd...he'd promised he would help me with this. With the school, to bring back the old ways."

"To bring back the Danann?" she said.

"When he became so fervently Christian, it was a shock to me. I'd counted on him for so much, and he chose to forget."

She carded the wool but didn't look at me. "So now, you think he owes it to you? The past? Whatever it is he promised?"

"Yes. He does. He remembers. He knows who he is. Yet he continues to deny..."

"Brigid, do you expect so much of him?" Dar asked. I heard the scolding in her tone.

"Yes, I do." I threw my unfinished wool into the basket. He was the one who called for me. He brought himself into my dreams since childhood. My expectations were as he set them.My head ached with the effort of remembering the past, my other past. Time shouldn't matter. Not with us. My heart ached, empty, hollow. The core of my soul was missing a central piece, whatever I was that made me complete. It was a place only Patrick could fill.

CHAPTER 24

Brigid

Conleth and I argued in the vestry while four guests waited in the courtyard. The conflict we'd tip-toed around now exploded. I had a unique position at Cill Dara. We disagreed often on how the school should be run, even over the fundamental task of a supply order. Now, we disagreed on formalities shown to visitors. I was tired of keeping the druids a secret. Mel didn't leave us with any instruction, expecting us to work it out for ourselves.

Rain beat down on the thatched roof, and the whitewashed walls were damp. Conleth paced back and forth in front of a trunk of new robes, recently arrived from Britannia. He guarded the new supply of garments, lest I snatch them in a mad dash and start giving the white robes away to strangers again.

"You can't go out there and pretend you are the bishop of Cill Dara," he said.

"Mel ordained me bishop," I retorted. "Others assume, incorrectly, my beliefs follow."

"You don't try to correct them."

"If you allowed visitors to witness a druid ceremony, or speak with me individually, they would understand how we co-exist."

"I show them the healing lodge and the metallurgy classes," he said.

I stood in front of the door, blocking it. He stepped to the left to go past me and I pressed my arm against the door. "You don't tell them we are druids, do you? You allow the priests to believe we are local smiths from Dun Ailenn." That was the problem. His problem. The druid half of the school was something he wanted to cover up. I'd overlooked a lot of his faults due to his broken hand and more recent trauma on the battlefield.

He pulled at his hair. "I thought we weren't supposed to let people know you were a druid. You're supposed to be hiding from your tribe or something."

"I'm not hiding. They know where I am. They can't legally take me from it. You hide the true nature of Cill Dara from everyone." Blood rushed to my face, and I took several deep breaths in an attempt to control my temper.

"The true nature? What is that? We are Cill Dara, *Church* of the Oak." He pounded his fist on the whitewashed wall, as if it proved his point.

"Cill Dara, Church of the *Oak*," I emphasized. "The oak, as you know, is sacred to druids." Exasperated, I wiped my brow. The summer heat and rain damp penetrated the stuffy room where we'd enclosed ourselves. Conleth threw his arms in the air, infuriated.

"You can't keep me from greeting guests and attending meetings," I said. "Those discussions affect all the members of this school, whether you recognize the druids or not."

"Brigid, you order supplies because Mel, in his infinite drunken wisdom, thought it would be in good form to put you in charge," Conleth said.

"I don't," I growled through clenched teeth, "just order supplies. The direction the Church decides for the school affects the druids. We were here first."

"Here we go again."

"The druids were here first," I ignored his interruption. "We kindly allowed Bishop Mel to build a church next door, and then he put you in charge of it."

"You needed Church protection, Brigid. You needed them to buy the land. Don't try to put yourself in a more favorable light. Mel told me about Maithghean and Dubhtach and their plans. If you need protection from slavery, fine, I wouldn't deny you that. But you can't pretend you have something in common with the priests who come to visit." Stonily, we glared at each other as four priests from Britannia waited outside.

"I'm going to greet them," I said. I sidled out the door before Conleth could stop me.

Conleth's eyes burned through me during the entire meeting. He was incensed. He thought I met the priests as if I were a Christian abbess and bishop. I never said that I was. Visitors often made their own assumptions.

"We would like qualified priests from Éire and Britannia to accompany us to Rome next year." Father Anthony believed a pilgrimage from the isle would gain the Pope's notice. "We would prefer priests and monks without families, such as you, Conleth. It is more difficult for those of us with wives and children to be away for so long."

"What message do you plan on sending to the Pope?" I asked.

"We want to bring the success of our conversions to Pope Celestine," he said. "He regularly favors the churches of Gaul and Rome, of course. We here on the edge of the world would like some attention as well." He smiled at me, as if I agreed with his statements.

"Do you think the conversions are successful?" I asked.

"Of course. This school is growing as well as many others."

"What I meant to say is, are they long lasting?" I asked. "The druid presence is a force to be reckoned with in Éire. All the Christian conversions might be a short-lived trend."

Conleth cocked his eyebrow at me, a silent warning that I said too much. Father Anthony shifted on his bench, as did his cohorts.

Conleth intervened. "Christianity takes on a unique form in Éire," he said. "As you know, Patrick in Armagh has strongly led the movement here."

"Pah!" Father Anthony made a dismissive gesture with his hand. "Patrick is not respected in Britannia. We need to bring new men to Rome, to show the Pope we aren't all dissenters."

"Patrick, a dissenter?" I knew Patrick made the Britannia leadership angry, but I wanted to hear it from them.

"He had no permission to come here years ago. Since then, we have seen little of his tithes. Rumor is he keeps it all to himself," Anthony smirked.

"Patrick wouldn't steal," I said. "The people he ministers to are poor, they are slaves. There isn't much to send." I knew the fidelity he pledged to the Church. I disagreed with his message, but I wouldn't have him thought of as a thief.

"Do you align yourself with him, Abbess?" Anthony asked. The other priests perked up with interest. I was on dangerous ground.

"No, I don't. If you must know, Father, I'm not aligned with - "

"It is time for us to show you the hospitality of our monastery," Conleth interrupted. He indicated for the men to follow him outdoors. "Let us convene for today, and go to the church where we may pray for a successful journey to Rome."

We left the main meeting hall and walked through driving rain into the chapel. The monks were repairing a final passageway that connected the vestry and a church entrance. Until that work was complete, we had to walk around to the front. Conleth had not let me purchase more wood from Dun Ailenn, nor did he request additional monks to help in the remodeling. As rain dripped down the faces of our guests, I gave him a look that said I told you so.

We were soaked, encumbered by the heavy wet wool of our cloaks and cowls. The monks were grateful for the shelter of the church, and I studied the flame outside in the courtyard, still alight in this weather.

The men knelt to pray, and I knelt at a pew as well. With utmost concentration, I sent my thoughts to Lugh and asked for the sun. He heard. I felt the earth shift beneath my feet. His energy rose through me. Lugh's light flowed in and warmed the damp walls of the chapel. The sudden change in weather broke the priests' prayer. They opened their eyes to the streaming golden rays.

I removed my blue cloak, wet from our walk through the rain, and focused all of my energy on the rays of sunlight that came through the window. I wanted to show them what druids could do. What the Danann could do. I wanted them to see what they denied. Druids wouldn't leave this land. The Danann wouldn't leave this land. We were part of it. I grounded into the earth. Power soared through me, into my very bones.

The men gasped and their eyes widened.

"Brigid?" Conleth's voice was tremulous.

"Your cloak!" Anthony exclaimed, as the blue woolen cloak stayed suspended, held aloft by the ray of light. Even Conleth seemed impressed, although I explained to him the simplicity of calling energy many times.

"This is my prayer," I said. "Light is my god, the sun, the earth, and the mists that fall from the sky. This is how all of Éire once prayed, before the church intervened."

I retrieved my cloak from the sunbeam, breaking the line of energy that held it. The men stirred, unsure of what they had just seen. I led them outdoors to the perpetual fire that blazed in its copper cauldron. The sun disappeared behind another cloud and a light mist fell.

"This flame is an ancient gift from our founders, the original gods and goddesses of Éire, those that represent the earth and the sun," I explained. "It is a reminder to us that they are still present." Even in the mist, the fire stayed lit.

Anthony smiled. "Ingenious, Brigid. You have completed a difficult task, drawing in the pagan element onto Christian grounds."

"What?" I asked, not understanding his reference.

"You have gained the druids, trust and enticed them here, onto Christian ground. What a wonderful plan for conversion. We must tell the Pope of this idea, of befriending the enemy. Brother Conleth, is this your doing? A subtle plot to house the druids on Christian soil, in order to convert them to the Church more effectively?" He glanced at Conleth, who stared up to the heavens, as if wishing he were anywhere else.

"No sir, it was Bishop Mel's idea," he answered honestly. A mixture of anger and failure flooded through me. I had been playing a game, straddling both druid and Christian worlds, and suddenly, it backfired.

"No," I interrupted. "I lead a school of druids, guided by the light of Lugh and the goddess Danu. There are no plans for conversion."

The flame dimmed, then flared again, even as mist gave way to rain again. The priests gasped at the strengthening lick of orange. A memory. The past power. The landscape swirled around me. I wavered, reached for something to grasp as I fell to the ground. Conleth caught me and prevented my head from crashing onto the flagstone path.

"Brigid? Brigid, answer me."

The priests hovered around, but Conleth waved them away.

"Brother Thomas," he called to a nearby monk. "Refresh our visitors with ale and cheese."

"Is she ill?" Anthony asked.

"Ah, no," stumbled Conleth. "Occasionally...the holy spirit...the power of our Lord overcomes the Abbess."

Brother Thomas led the flabbergasted men to the kitchen.

"Brigid?" Conleth whispered. "Enough play acting for the priests. They are gone now."

I stayed in his arms, unable to move.

CHAPTER 25
Patrick and Brigid

P atrick ran outside, outraged, away from the confines of walls. On the hill of Armagh, he took great gulps of clean air in an effort to control his rage. He'd baptized the innocent souls at the Easter feast, an event which rivaled the fires of Beltane. Some fifty people, including women and children, donned white robes in honor of Christ's resurrection. Patrick, weeks before, had left the celebration early to prepare for next day's Mass. His eyes filled with tears, as he clutched the branches of a nearby oak. They were good people, honest, in need of the Lord and accepting of his love, whom he anointed only days before. Damn Coroticus!

As the new converts celebrated their faith on the coastal hillsides, a British pirate, Coroticus, attacked them unaware. He hunted for slaves, taking the valuable women and children as captives, and viciously murdering the men. Patrick escaped the scene by only a few hours.

"I can't stand by and do nothing," Patrick said aloud. With long legged strides, he returned to his office and grabbed a quill and parchment. He sat down to write.

"I'm Patrick the ignorant sinner and, I declare, a bishop in Ireland, a position I believe I was appointed to by God himself..." He paused in a moment of self-doubt. What power would he have over this evil pirate, who claimed himself a prince in Britannia? Coroticus might listen to the bishops of Britannia...well, given his horrendous actions, probably not. I declare myself Bishop of Éire, Patrick thought, although the Church has yet to formalize my post. He recalled his hasty departure from Auxerre when the voice called to him. An angel, he told his followers. An angel with clover scent and copper hair. It had not been a man's voice who spoke his name. With intense concentration, he turned his attention back to his Latin writing, perspiration forming on his brow.

"... I sent a message to you with a priest I taught from childhood and some other clergy asking that you return the surviving captives with at least some of their goods, but you only laughed."

A priest, accompanied by his warrior guards from the nearby fort, sent Patrick the news as almost as quickly as it happened. When the priest begged him to release the prisoners, Coroticus laughed in his face. He took them just as the Irish had taken his British neighbors. Patrick ought to know, Coroticus said to the terrified priest. Then Coroticus steered his ship toward the British coast.

What sickened Patrick the most was that Coroticus claimed to be a Christian. He was no pagan Irish king that Patrick could easily denounce, but one of his own, a Christian Briton who kidnapped the Irish for slavery in Britannia.

"You," he wrote, "you kill them or sell them as slaves to people who don't even know God. It's as if you sold your fellow Christians to a brothel."

Patrick wept now, imagining the small faces of children who would be doomed to a lifetime of cruelty, by his own British people. He knew the rape and abuse the women would face, remembering his childhood friends Lupida and Darceca. I was lucky, he realized. I escaped, with the grace of God, while most people remained enslaved. In his travels, he searched for the two women, but he had yet to find them.

He bent his head in prayer, a fervent plea for the Irish women and children taken by Coroticus of Britannia, and the souls of the men, now resting with God.

He completed his letter and hastily wrote out copies. Coroticus alone wouldn't heed his call to free his captives. If there were pressure from other priests and bishops in Britannia, however, perhaps the abominable practice would end.

"I implore you, those among you who are servants of God, be courageous and deliver this letter everywhere..."

Patrick reread his harsh words. He cringed as he reviewed his words toward the Picts: "You live like the worst barbarians, including your Pictish friends..." Many Picts were slaves in Éire, and several had turned to God, such as Brocca, Brigid's mother. He'd met the small dark woman before, blessing new Christians in smaller settlements to the south. Patrick recognized the fine bone structure she shared with her daughter...Enough, he told himself. He read his letter again, wincing at his Latin, finding mistakes where there were none. If the Picts, or any tribes, engaged in the slave trade, they deserved to be called wicked and godless. He finished copying his final letter, his hand cramped, and called in his most trusted monk.

"Cross the sea. Deliver these into the hands of the Bishop and any priests you can find. We must try to free the people Coroticus captured."

"Do you think it will work, Father?" the monk asked reluctantly. Patrick knew he wouldn't be overjoyed about a mission that sent him over stormy waters to follow a murderous pirate.

"I don't know. We have to try." Patrick left his office and headed to the church to pray in peace for the lost souls.

He knelt behind the pew. His bony knees ached on the hard stone floor. It didn't matter. He was not in the church for his own physical comfort. The emotional toll of the recent days left him drained. He'd traveled for weeks, turned away by many, but accepted by those reverent few, glorious in their white baptismal robes. His monk delivered one of the robes to him, found on the roadside, stained with blood.

He no longer possessed the strength to pray any longer for his newest converts, so brutalized by Coroticus, now either dead or enslaved. Writing tired him as well, his Latin poor and incomplete. He worried his letters would have no effect. After all, Coroticus was an evil man, but still a British citizen. Patrick himself was a poor priest in Éire, and his British roots may not matter. Long ago, he gave up any claim to his prestigious birth. He sighed and leaned his aching head on the bench in front of him, eyes closed. He languished in the silence, appreciating the fleeting calm, and drifted into the hazy place between sleep and wakefulness.

Help me! She cried as she was downwards. He ran to her, watching with revulsion as she began to meld with the earth, her body becoming an impression in the green grass and loamy soil.

"Brigid, take my hand." He reached out to her.

"I'm trying," she said. "They are pulling me back. They are angry with us, Patrick. We have failed them." Her coppery hair flowed beneath the grass, like roots

taking hold. Eerily, only her green eyes stared up at him, like emeralds peering out of the black earth.

His heart beat rapidly, terrified of losing her to the underground depths. If she were gone, he couldn't survive.

"Don't let go," he pleaded, as her hand slipped from his. Their strength, combined, was more than his was. White-hot anger rose within him. "I broke the promise," he said. "Take me. Don't punish her for my faults." He swung his legs over the edge of sunken earth, prepared to go to the Danann caves, instead of Brigid.

"No, Patrick, you don't know what you're saying." Arching, she pushed against him, pushing him upwards, away from the Danann. He struggled on the edge, determined not to let Brigid fall. He reorganized his grip, clasping both of her hands in his. As their hands held, his energy flowed into her, willing her to remain with him. She lifted slightly from the earth, as the Danann lost their connection.

With stunning force, he pulled her back, and they both lay breathless on a mountainside and gripped on to the solidity of the quartzite boulder.

"They can't take me when you are here. Why is that?" she asked. "Padraic, How do you always keep me with you?"

Patrick didn't answer. He didn't know. He knew he had come dangerously close to losing her. She reached her hand to him. "Stay with me, stay," he murmured. They clutched each other tightly. Their survival depended on each other.

Patrick raised his head, dazed, as darkness fell inside the church.

"Brigid? Take my hand." The words were comforting and his grip, warm.

Wrenched into the present, I clung to the blanket in my hand and clasped for anything solid. The wool felt odd, for I expected sharp-edged quartz instead. Conleth peered over me, and the branches of the oak swayed behind him.

I tried to speak but couldn't. My mouth was dry. I struggled to stand, to go toward the rushing water I heard from the nearby river.

"No, Brigid. Stay here with me," said Conleth. I tried to stand again, overcome with dizziness. "Stay here. You're too tired to walk."

I listened to his words, Patrick's words. Tears welled in my eyes, slipped down my cheeks. The voice, present and dream, melded into one. Where was he?

Conleth fumbled with a bag tied to his belt. He put the opening to my mouth, and I sipped earthy red wine.

"What happened?" I asked, although I knew better than Conleth what took place. The Túatha de Danann tried to take me back, to pull me under, in their fury at me for failing them. They almost succeeded, except for Patrick. Again, he was there. Again, he saved me.

"You fainted, and I brought you here, under the shade. You continued to..." Conleth stopped, confused.

"Sink?" I finished for him.

"Yes," he nodded. "You were... descending... somehow, but I caught hold of your hands. I pulled you back." He ran his palm over the indentation of earth next to me, trying to make logical sense of the mystery. He stared at his hands, twice now the ministers of actions he didn't assign.

The summery oak leaves glinted and wavered in the sunlight. Conleth said he pulled me out, held my hands. It was Patrick who saved me, not Conleth. We were not here, under the oak, but somewhere far to the west, clinging to the quartzite stone, far on a mountainside.

"Please get Dar for me," I whispered. She would understand. Conleth ran to do my bidding.

CHAPTER 26

Brigid

Conleth and I reviewed inventory and counted the number of new robes for the monks, nuns, and druids. The plain wool robes had been woven by nuns and druids. I counted out the pots of dye for the necessary colors, woad for the druid's blue, and madder for the monk's coarse brown. Conleth's hand brushed mine as we reached for the same robe. I glanced up to find his eyes intent upon me.

"Brigid..." His hand stilled next to mine.

I shook my head at his unexpected action. "No, Conleth, you can't..." My voice trailed off as I saw the eagerness and hope deep in his eyes. I stood frozen, taken by surprise. I liked Conleth, perhaps more than I cared to admit. I was drawn to him, in spite of, or maybe because of, our disagreements. He had a kindness that shone through, and there was the solidity of his presence. A brief pang resonated in me as I thought of Patrick, far to the north, bound to his vows.

Conleth kept his fingertips against my wrist, as if waiting for a response. He was a kind man, an honorable man, not attached to idealistic promises brought on by guilt. He wanted things of the earth, a home, and family. I closed my eyes and thought of those dreams I once shared with Padraic...Patrick.

Melwyn toddled into the vestry, looking for a sweet. No part of the grounds, druid or Christian, were off limits to the little girl adopted by the whole community. I left Conleth's side and rummaged through a basket of food I'd brought for our long workday. I dipped a piece of bread in honey for her and was grateful for the opportunity to look away and gather my swirling thoughts. I picked up the baby girl. She smacked happily on her sticky treat. She was strong and healthy, and at almost two years old, healed from the wasting cough that nearly killed her.

"Brigid?" Conleth walked to us and brushed his hand shyly across my brow. He traced his finger from my face to Melwyn's. I shivered with attraction, physical touch missing from my life for far too long.

"Conleth, I'll be honest with you." I said. "I do care for you." He smiled so broadly I almost didn't continue. "But, my heart belongs elsewhere. You must know this before anything else."His brow furrowed. Who? I read the question on his face. "No one here, and no one who shares my feelings." That wasn't completely true. I believed Patrick did share my feelings but he chose a different path for his life. I looked away and fussed with the little girl in my arms instead. What Patrick and I shared was beyond simple emotion. Tied together beyond our borders, beyond time, yet we would never make love, have a family, or spend winters warmed by the fire of a shared hearth. Patrick had chosen his path for this lifetime.

Conleth's rough wool alb grazed against my arm, and his breath was warm on my face as he came close.

"You do care for me? There could be more, someday?" he asked. Someday...the word pierced through me. I studied Conleth, his broad face and fair hair so different from...it didn't matter. I was tired of the otherworldly interference and intertwined fates I couldn't control. I wanted something real, solid. I allowed warmth to build from within, letting my attraction to Conleth grow. His lips brushed mine gently.

Melwyn giggled, and Conleth pulled away with a smile.

"The two of you there, so beautiful in the light," he whispered.

I imagine he saw a Madonna-like scene, me with Melwyn in my arms. I returned his smile. He was my friend. I could be content with him, despite our surface disagreements. I appreciated the goodness and simplicity of his soul. I put Melwyn down and sent her outside to find Dar then closed the door to the vestry. I turned to find a warm and kind man waiting. I took his face in my hands and kissed him again, trying to fill what had been empty for so long.

We fumbled in our relationship at first, neither of us knowing how to meet on the school and church grounds. Yet we were free in a different way, not bound to any rules or standards. None of what we knew applied at Cill Dara. We began slowly. To start, we took walks in the evening until sunset.

"Tell me about leaving your tuath for the Christian community." I was curious about his family's experience compared to my mother's.

"My father died. We could have received the warrior's compensation. My mother could have married again and kept her rank, but she chose to leave. She'd met traveling Christians and accepted their beliefs. She wanted to start a new life."

"Was it difficult? Leaving?" I thought of the troubles Brocca went through, the permission she needed to break from Dubhtach.

He shook his head. "I was young. I was more upset about my father's death." Conleth held my hand as we walked. "I guess I was homesick for a while, when we first arrived. Then it was a peaceful community. A simple life of shared faith. No war. No battles."

We sat along the riverbank. "You left your home. Don't you miss it?" He asked.

"I thought that I would, but I don't," I said. "With my mother gone and Dubhtach becoming what he has, no. I had to leave."

"Maybe our school, our monastery, provides new homes for all of us. A chance for escape, for something new."

"Maybe you're right." I leaned against his shoulder, comforted by his unyielding strength. We all had to escape for one reason or another. Escape. Patrick. I closed my eyes, angry that all my thoughts led to him. "Come, Conleth. It's late. We should get back."

He pulled me back to him. "Stay until dark." He kissed my neck.

I stood. I recognized what I had done. Whether Conleth knew it or not, I brought Patrick with us. I set the barrier. It was mine.

We continued our walks on other nights. I always wanted to be the first to return to Cill Dara, even though I enjoyed our conversations. We talked about our beliefs, about how Cill Dara was becoming a blend, a blurred line between Christian and druid. Nuns trained with me in the healing arts. Druids learned the art of illumination, trying their hand at combining colors and creating shapes, spirals, and serpents. Since freeing myself from Fotharit, I was able to examine my own beliefs and see what shape they took. I found there to be a continuum of Christian beliefs, with Patrick on one extreme and Conleth in the middle. Some druids, Ean in particular, were angry that apprentices learned to write on parchment.

"Our bards tell our families histories from memory, and that is all," Ean argued.

"Why can't they write it?" I asked. "What harm does it do? The things we need to remember are based on the teachings of the Ancients: how to be one with Danu, with the earth and the rivers. What about those things, Ean?"

He didn't answer, but had turned on his heel to go back to Dun Ailenn.

My animosity toward the Christians lessened. How could I stay angry? Our druids refused to go back to the ancient ways, and, so far, only Dar, Cecilia, and I came close to connecting with the Danann. Bishop Mel, on the other hand, gave me a place of safe haven. Dar and I taught as we chose. Unity is what will hold Éire together, I reflected. *What of us?* The Danann cries sometimes woke me in the night. I had no answer for them

The river was the one place where Conleth and I found privacy. Students at both schools began to speculate about our relationship, but I had no intention of making it obvious. Dar knew, of course, but I spoke to her little about it. I had to work out our beliefs, our similarities and our differences, is what I told her. We both knew I had to quell my dreams of Patrick.

I'd gained new respect for Conleth, the man I called my friend. He truly believed in his call to God and preferred the simplicity of the new faith. He shook his head at the elaborate rituals of Samhain and Solstice as I explained them one night as we sat by the river. "I know the rituals and was raised with them. But now, I don't need to sacrifice animals or dance in circles to speak to the Lord," he said.

"You take communion each week. You believe it is the body of your Christ. Why is that so different from a sacrifice at Samhain?" I countered his argument, not to dissuade him, but to understand.

"The Bread and Cup are not animals. They are part of the Lord, part of the Creator."

"As are our sacrifices. They are a part of Danu, our Goddess, our Creator."

On those incongruent points, we found a thin line of agreement.

Conleth and I spent our days at work, teaching a myriad of students on our respective sides of the school. Two druid apprentices began to work in the healer's garden while Conleth managed an influx of several new monks and nuns. I tried to push back the bite of jealousy I felt as the monastery at Cill Dara grew faster than the druid school. True, some of my students were also nuns, but that fact didn't blind me to the stark realization the druid numbers had decreased.

"We are doing what we can," said Dar as we compared our numbers with the Christians. I took my place next to her in front of the hearth. We often sat side by side on the bench, reviewing our day, our classes, our students.

"Do you see it?" I asked. "Our lack of support isn't random. Druids are dwindling."

Her laugh was dry. "We helped create that, you know."

I knew. The school that I had dreamed of had transformed into something unexpected.

The fire burned bright, that element I could control if I chose. I reach toward it, to draw it to me. If the people could see what they could do, the power we all contained, somewhere, within...

"Brigid..." Dar's voice was soft now. "We can travel for new students this summer. We'll go west."

"Perhaps." The flame reached toward me, my fingers to its orange tip. Then the heat pulled back and settled into the embers. The Ancient Ones have left us. "We've lost."

"No," said Dar. "We've changed."

"We have."

"Not completely. We still have students. I still teach the seer's work. How goes it with Conleth?" asked Dar.

"He's a good man. He has a kind heart."

She handed me a mug of chamomile and looked at me in the way she had. She knew I held back. A best friend as a visionary was difficult. I couldn't hide from her. "You know what it is, Dar. You know why I can't give myself to him completely."

"Even so," she said. "You should have your own home. We have the space now, with so few students. I can move into one of the roundhouses."

I thought Conleth and I had been discreet. We met outdoors or in his house. Our first time making love together was warm, comfortable. He was my friend, and I enjoyed our closeness. I blocked Patrick from my mind, blocked the memories of our meeting between worlds when I was goddess and not-goddess. If I could train my mind to focus on the present, on Conleth's sturdy and strong builder's hands caressing my skin.

Conleth and I celebrated Beltane quietly, privately in his house, and we watched the bonfires glow far into the distance.

"Do you want to go to the bonfires, Brigid?" he asked.

"Would you want to go?"

"No. But that's not what I wanted to know. I don't want to be the one stopping you from..."

I leaned up on my elbow, from where I lay next to him. "Really, Conleth? You would be fine if I celebrated Beltane the old way?" I recalled Patrick and I watching the fires from the mountain top so many years ago. Celebrating in teh old way.

"I would not, honestly. But I don't want you to be here because you have to be..."

"We accept our differences. We find what we have in common instead," I whispered back, feeling a contentment I had not felt in a long time. His arms were strong around me. I cherished his warmth and strength. "And you know Beltane is more than the dancing and the coupling. It's celebrating new marriages."

"Why are we not out by the bonfires, then?" he asked. "Why are we not making our vows, our commitment to a life together?"

I stiffened. There it was again. Conleth wanted more than I could give. I could be with Conleth in the present, but I couldn't imagine a future with him – children, a life together. All of that blended into Patrick. A past so long ago it seemed to be a dream. A stupid dream to hold onto, but it was ingrained in me. Patrick was ingrained in me. Part of me.

"I don't think your Church would accept our marriage."

"We're allowed to marry, Brigid. Many monks are married, even here. You know that. Several are married in Erc's community. Some of the bishops in Armagh talk about changing the rules, but it is all talk. They're more concerned about paying for housing for wives and children." He waved his hand, dismissing the movement Patrick had begun.

"Are you allowed to marry druids?" I asked. I looked for any argument I could find. "It's fine if Christians marry, but this is different."

"Half the land thinks you're the Abbess of Cill Dara. Does it matter? Brigid, I want to be with you."

"You are with me. Nothing would change, Conleth."

He sighed and turned away. His tight embrace around me was gone. "The only thing stopping us, Brigid, is you."

"You know why. I have been honest with you from the beginning. I don't understand how you still want me, knowing my heart belongs to another..." I had let myself believe Conleth accepted the parameters of my affection, but he didn't know my past with Patrick, Padraic, which was too complicated to explain. At times, I didn't understand it.

"That mysterious other." Conleth left the bed and returned with a pitcher of water. "You won't tell me who, and that's fine. I don't think I want to know." He handed me a mug, and I was glad for the distraction. "There are different kinds of love. There are different kinds of happiness. We could be happy, Brigid, if you let us."

CHAPTER 27

Brigid

Conleth received a notice from Armagh. He ran to me, excited. Patrick would visit Cill Dara to inspect the grounds of the growing Christian community. "Patrick is coming here. It's an honor."

I grew nervous at the prospect of seeing Patrick again and curious as to why he would inspect our school. Cill Dara fell under Mel's domain. "Will you explain to him what our school truly encompasses, Conleth? Explain how we accept one another?" We'd worked hard to come to an agreement about our school to end the petty arguments. Conleth and I began to take pride in the fact we had created a school where both beliefs co-existed. Now that line seemed to waver, with Patrick's impending visit.

"I will speak of your druid instruction, Brigid," Conleth said. "I do wish for Patrick's approval. He is an admirable man, and his opinion does matter to me."

"What if he doesn't agree with our philosophy? What if he doesn't think druids should be here at all?" I didn't know what Patrick believed anymore. Images of him jumbled in my brain. He was the devout priest who sacrificed all. He met me in my dreams and saved me time and again from the ancient forces below. He was Padraic of the past, Patrick of the present.

"Do you think he would be so harsh, Brigid?" Conleth and I found two flat stones along the riverside and sat together.

"He may be. Cill Dara is distinctive. You saw how Father Anthony reacted, even when I blurted out the truth. He does not hold the druids in any esteem. We must be sure Patrick knows we believe in unity, that both beliefs can and will exist in

Éire." Patrick - Padraic - was of the Danann, as I was. I clung to this, no matter how far in the past it was.

"Patrick will be entitled to his own opinion, of course. A man of his knowledge and experience will understand what we are trying to do. Why do you think he won't understand this?" Conleth skipped a pebble across the flowing waters. This point of conversation was tricky for us. Although we both respected the other's tradition, it was more difficult when visitors were involved. Conleth believed in an individual choice to convert, whereas many of his brothers felt it was necessary to bring the religion to each village and fort. His personal philosophy, possibly at my influence, sometimes put him in an uncomfortable situation.

The green banks of the river rose up around us and sheltered us from prying eyes. I leaned back on the boulder, focusing on the clear water, which glinted with gold from the sun. I ran my hand along sandstone beneath me, comforted by its solidity.

"I don't know," I answered, listening to the rush of the stream as it polished age-old stones. "I've heard Patrick is very strict. I think we should be prepared for any response."

"It will be fine, Brigid. You're more worried about his visit than I am." He smiled and stood, pulling me up with him. With an unexpected flourish, he lifted me and spun me around on top of our river rocks. Conleth kissed me as his laughter rang across the river.

CHAPTER 28

Brigid

"Welcome to Cill Dara." I greeted Patrick and his retinue of monks. Dar stood by my side and Conleth stepped forth to extend his hands. We prepared for weeks, and a feast waited for our guests after general introductions and a brief tour of the school. Our table was laden with roasted pig stuffed with apples and loaves of brown bread and fresh butter. The monks rolled out barrels of ale in their casks, and the nuns and druids stacked wheels of cheese for our company. I was proud of our domain, nuns and monks and pagans, who had learned to coexist in peace. It wasn't my original intention for the school, but I was glad for what it had become.

Patrick's blue eyes were unchanged, though his hair was streaked with white. It was the first time I'd seen him since my journey to Armagh. No, that is untrue, I thought. I saw him often in my dreams and visions.

"Abbess," Patrick addressed me formally.

Several of his monks shifted from one foot to another, and their eyes darted around with furtive glances. They looked closely at the druids' dark blue dresses and robes, dyed with woad, as though they tried to decipher if we were nuns and monks, or not. Mariah and her nuns had robes similar to ours, except without the hood.

"I will show you the church and scrolls completed by our monks," Conleth explained. "Brigid will give you a tour of our community first, and then she'll direct you to our chapel and vestry, where we can discuss specific issues."

Conleth and I scripted each step of our tour for Patrick. Conleth grasped my fingers in his as he left to place the most impressive scrolls and writings on display.

Surreptitiously, I brushed his hand away. This was a formal visit, after all, from the man who considered himself Bishop of Éire in the north. This was no time for romance. My face burned with my own lie to myself. I didn't push Conleth away because of etiquette.

Patrick and I walked through Cill Dara. My hands shook with nerves, and I hid them in the pockets of my skirt. Stop being ridiculous, I thought. Did he still see me in his dreams? I was sure he did. If I had the dreams, so did he. I wanted to ask him, but his monks accompanied him, and Dar and Mariah stayed by my side.

Patrick remained aloof as I explained the charity works done at Cill Dara, by both Christian and druid. "We care for the sick that can't find help in their homes. Often one of our healers will visit the countryside to administer medicines."

"Mariah and several of the nuns also know the healing arts," he said.

"They do. Now. Because I taught them. They didn't stop that child's wasting cough." Melwyn ran in front of us, under the watchful eyes of two nuns. I created tinctures for her cough, and Dar stayed with her for days until she was well. Mariah now continued to make special teas for her. "Your Christian nuns were willing to leave her in the cold, believing she was a changeling, a fairy child"

"Let me see," Patrick reached down and picked up the girl. The edges of his eyes crinkled with his smile.

"How has she fared?" he asked the nuns.

"She's done well, Father. Brigid, Dar, and Sister Mariah nursed her back to health." The nuns smiled and blushed in Patrick's presence. His charisma, I noted, affected many women at Cill Dara.

"So, are you a fairy, little Melwyn?" he asked as he tossed her gently in the air. She giggled. "There's no such thing as fairies."

"Really?" He looked sideways at me. "No such thing as fairies?" He handed her back to the nuns. I smiled when our eyes met. There was a brief moment when his humor shone through, a Danann connection, before his bishop's mask returned.

"You will find many students of both faiths making jewelry and metalwork." I showed him the cluster of buildings, heated by forges. Druid and monk hammered out sturdy, useful tools, as well as fine decorations made of gold. Cecilia showed us her newest creation, interlaying gold wire into a dagger handle with spirals and serpents. Patrick nodded, unimpressed. We continued, and I walked on, frustrated. I wanted some reaction from him, some feedback that he recognized the powerful work we were doing.

"Conleth has been training the monks, as well as a few druids, in the art of illuminations. Druids, of course, focus on the art, the drawings, blending colors and inks. Monks also learn the written script." I stepped into the monks' hall. They sat in rows, and copied their Bible stories with elaborate designs to frame the page. Scrolls of vellum littered the tables, and inks and dyes led the eye to a riot of color on each script. The men at each bench, however, were silent, concentrating on their rendering of the verse.

"Why are only the Christians writing stories?" Patrick asked, in what I thought was a haughty tone. "If this is a school of dual learning, shouldn't the pagans copy the stories?"

"Which stories? Those from the Bible? Or those of the Danann?"

His face flushed red. He'd walked right into my forever sticking point. "Besides," I said. "You know druids don't trust the written word. All of our stories must be told from one generation to the next, by word of mouth," I paused. "You know that, Patrick."

Conleth joined me in the tour and guided the small of my back with his hand. Patrick caught the movement and his eyes flared. With a steady gaze, I met his anger. Why should I be denied what he refused to give? He looked away and turned his attention to Conleth as he pointed out a monk's intricate design on the Book of Matthew.

We continued our walk through the campus together. Conleth stayed close to my side, oblivious of the clench in Patrick's jaw. We three stepped into the darkened chapel, quiet and peaceful. I pointed to the flame outside in the courtyard.

"The flame is our source of meditation and prayer. Conleth and I designed the church so that the fire is visible through the window."

Patrick remained indifferent. "I'm not sure that Christ worshiped with fire," he said coolly.

"Candles light the altars of many churches," Conleth responded. He enjoyed a good debate as I well knew.

"The power of the flame comes from the earth, as does all druid power," I said. "It need not be sheltered."

Patrick turned to the both of us, puzzled. "Has Brigid influenced you, my Christian brother, to accept the pagan ways?"

Conleth's eyebrows shot up in surprise. Rarely did Christians outside of Cill Dara guess my true status.

"I remain faithful to God and Christ. However, I find no sin in fire, and if it brings the druids closer to my chapel, then so be it."

"It is a beautiful building, Conleth. A testament to God's work here in Éire."

Conleth beamed with the praise from the older man.

"We must see to the evening meal," I said. "I'll explain to Patrick the source of the fire." I promised I would bring Patrick to the hall. My words worked, and Conleth left to gather the Christian community into the main lodge.

Tension filled the chapel. Patrick kept his hands clasped behind his back, and I thought I saw sadness in his eyes.

Although I had been dubious of Mel's plan to share Cill Dara at first, I liked what the school had become. Cill Dara now was the perfect synthesis of Éire, a symbol of both beliefs in this land.

"How can you believe as you do, Brigid, yet take a leadership role here? I'm still confused."

"The Church knows I was raised pagan and accepted my appointment from Bishop Mel. Most everyone here is native Irish and was raised with the druid beliefs. I'm not sure why you think this is a problem."

"It's not that you were raised as a druid. It's that you continue to be one, yet call yourself Abbess."

"We've been through this, Patrick. I don't call myself by that title. Neither does anyone here. You did, though, when you arrived. Why did you? Was it a mistake?"

"Because that is how Mel ordained you. That is the title known to all church officials."

"Then you need to have this conversation with Mel, not with me. Any errors are his. Or yours."

"Mel is a drunken priest, too fond of his wine," Patrick said.

"Mel is my friend. He believes in me and in Cill Dara."

"You claim this place for God, yet you don't believe." His voice rose in frustration. "It's a farce." His words, like cold water, drenched my entire being.

"This is my life's work. It is not a farce," I hissed. "We agreed to share this land, and it's worked out for everyone here."

"You aren't a Christian!" he exclaimed, hands thrown skyward. "You're no Christian, but somehow you have Mel and Conleth convinced you are everything holy."

"Mel came to his own conclusions. You know what I believe. You also know why this deal was made. Have you ignored everything I've told you?"

We faced each other in front of the window, and the flame outside flickered between us. It grew dark and the chapel dimmed. Only the flame gave light.

"I don't understand how you can be both, Brigid. I don't understand my dreams, how you can be here now after you were gone for so long. I don't understand why you keep talking about the past - that past - and you call me Padraic." His words tumbled out in a rush. We sat in a pew, and I took his hands in mine. He grasped mine tightly, like in my dreams, as if he were afraid to fall over the edge.

"I told you, many years ago, about reincarnation, about spirits and souls that pass into a new life. We share that tie, Patrick."

He shook his head, as though he refused to hear my words.

"You don't have to believe in it," I continued. "It is the only way I can explain how I knew you then and that is how I'm here now."

"If that is true," he said, "then how can you justify your position with the Church?"

I sighed. This again. "I don't have to justify the assumption of others. Even so, our beliefs aren't mutually exclusive. God is wonderful, huge, and expansive. More than we can fathom." Conleth and I agreed on this completely. It was that mutual awe of the Creator, in whatever name he or she took, God, Goddess, Christ, or Danu, that held us together.

"We had a past together. We promised to fight for the Danann. We lived our lives together -"

He held up his hand, willing me to stop. Patrick closed his eyes and sighed. "When I hear you speak, I can almost believe what you say."

"Why not believe it?" I whispered. "What else is there?" He brought my hand to his face, and I stroked the roughness of his beard. My fingertips caught on the edge of his eyelashes. "Brigid...your voice reminds me of that summer together. Keep speaking."

I continued to speak, my hand still pressed in his. "Our mission here is to keep the old ways in the world. Please don't let them die away to a forgotten realm. You have the power to achieve this, Patrick. Your gift is great...my school here is only one small piece. You have reached many people, and you can reach more. You can tell them all gods can exist in harmony."

"I preach the Word of God as I know it," he said. Abruptly, his eyes opened.

"It is not all you know," I said. "You know the old gods as well as I."

"There is only One True God, Brigid. It is blasphemy to say otherwise." His voice cracked. A struggle was going on within him.

"It is blasphemy to deny the truth that others have existed. To deny that you existed...before...when we were together. Padraic..."

His struggle was visible as he tried to make sense of the confusion.

"What of Conleth?" Patrick gazed outside at the flame. A breeze blew, yet the fire remained.

"What of him?" I pulled away. I could not speak of Conleth while Patrick still held my hand.

"I see what is happening between you." He didn't look at me and watched the fire instead.

"It is not forbidden," I whispered.

"No, though I wish it were. I wish he didn't have the right to touch you." His hand gripped mine as if he wanted to disprove Conleth's existence.

"You chose your path, Patrick. You could always change it."

We fell into silence and I ached for him again. Our past. Our future. What was it that barred him from me?

"My dreams. I see you all the time. I reach for you, pull you away from danger. Other times..." His voice trailed off. Other times. Other dreams.

"I know," I replied. "You have, somehow, saved me, many times."

Tears filled the crags and lines of his face as he nodded with the memories. He turned to me with tortured eyes and plaintive voice. "Why?"

The light grew dim and the shadows of the chapel cast columns of darkness. I reached out to him again. "I don't know why or how. I wish that we could change this and be together."

"We can wish for nothing more. We can only accept what is." He glanced at me one last time as he rose and left the chapel.

CHAPTER 29

Patrick and Brigid

"They no longer call for you, do they?" Patrick asked when she met him on the mountain beside the quartzite slab, their secret place. She took his hand, which was flesh and not flesh, in the transitory place between waking and dreams.

"No, I've told them I share their wishes, but I will no longer do their bidding. I cannot live between two worlds." Yet, she did live between both.

"I will see you less and less. Even if the dreams with the Danann were horrifying, I saw you. I could hold you." He brought her hand to his lips, in secret awe of the spiritual realm they entered. Was it the ancient ones, he wondered? Or is it a work of God? Brigid understood the question in his mind. She didn't know either.

"You can hold me now." She leaned into him. "You don't need to wait for dreams. If you wake, you only need to walk to my door," she whispered.

"No," he said. "I will not wake. I told you of my promises. In the light of day, on the solid earth. Not here. Promises are all that I have. Éire is my life, as is my devotion to God."

"Then why do you seek me here? You meet me in the night. Isn't it as much of a sin as if we met in bed?"

"I don't seek you, I never have. I think of you, and it happens. We are here." He pointed over the slab of quartzite and the shimmering bay of water to the west.

He kissed her gently. It was not a sin here, in this hidden niche, displaced from the rest of the world. They kissed again, more urgently, the dream deed to complete before he awoke. His spirit drank its fill of her, yet he, the man, was not sated.

Patrick awoke alone, fully human and full of need.

Patrick's visit continued for another day. He listened to Conleth's homily and watched the monks copy their script, decorating each page with elaborate designs and colors. He avoided any further contact with the druids, gliding away from the weaving room, gardens, and healing lodge, anywhere I, or any druid, might be present.

I dreamed of Patrick, which distracted and confused me. We'd met on the quartzite rock, the place where he pulled me to safety from the Danann grasp. Yet, there were no Danann this time.

I thought of Conleth and our relationship. I hated hiding the truth about Patrick from him. It wasn't fair. Not now, with Patrick on Cill Dara's grounds. How could I tell Conleth about the connection that Patrick and I shared?

At our morning meal, I regarded Conleth and Patrick as they discussed church policy. They were outwardly very different, but inside, they both possessed a rare goodness of spirit.

Patrick was tall, angular with blue eyes that burned as he surveyed a room. He chafed under the rules sent forth by the Britannia bishops, declaring Éire needed her own path and place in the Church hierarchy. I was proud of his determination.

Conleth was shorter, stockier and his friendly, open face busily absorbed the scene surrounding him. Enamored with Patrick, he spent the meal listening to his words, nodding in agreement over several points.

Guiltily, I left the hall, unable to watch both men before me. Conleth was good, caring, and kind. Yet, he was not Patrick. I didn't have the past with him, the bond that carried us through over time. Unfair, I thought to myself. Conleth cares for me. He loves me. I sighed, and wished I could muster the same depth of feeling for him.

Simple tasks were what I needed to calm myself and sort out my emotions. I brushed off Dar's concerned look and sought my refuge in the barn. Tucked into the safety of the dairy shed, I headed to my favorite brown cow. I grabbed the milk pails and began to work. Streaming milk hit the pail in regular syncopation, a breaking rhythm in the quiet. I understood how my mother received her comfort in the solitude of the stables.

Footsteps, hushed and inquisitive, entered the shed. Patrick: I was sure of it before I saw him, his height crouched under the stone lintel.

"Do you love him?" He asked without preamble.

"I care for him. Conleth is a good man."

"He is." He watched my hands work under the cow. "What of a future? Marriage?"

"I don't know yet," I answered.

"You dreamed again, didn't you? Last night?" He asked as stoked the cow gently on her head and then paced around the confining stall. His pacing made the cow anxious, and I motioned him away. He walked over to study a pair of lambs at the end of the stable.

"It is a torment to both of us," he said. "Those dreams." He knelt before the lambs as the mother ewe crowded protectively.

"They are not my doing, Patrick. I swear to you, they are not something within my control."

Tentatively, he put his hand into the pen and touched the lambs on their moist noses. He leaned in to lift a small lamb and stroked her downy ears.

"I've dreamed of you all my life," I whispered. "Even when I was a child. The dreams are all I have of you. I don't want them to end."

He returned the lamb to the pen.

"Nor do I, Brigid. The dreams of you are all I have as well." He left the stables, as quietly as he entered.

CHAPTER 30

Brigid

I sprinkled pepper on my thin gruel, a combination of chicken fat and a few late harvest carrots. The spice was rare, a gift from Rome. Occasionally, those far away spices reached Conleth and he shared with all of us. Steam rose before me as I sipped it, grateful for the warmth against the cold chill of winter.

Hunger ravaged the land again and our food supplies were depleted. We gave to those who knocked on our door, those who had less than we, and now the monastery's cupboards were bare. The black spice was a welcome diversion for my dulled tongue.

The messenger collapsed with cold and exhaustion in front of the fire in my study. I banked it, adding fuel to keep the boy warm and laid a woolen wall hanging over him. It would do no good to disturb him.

A cloud of warmth surrounded my face as I drained the last drops from the wooden bowl. I set it aside and contemplated the sealed letter before me, a missive from Britannia. I lifted it toward the light and saw the Latin script.

Father taught me the Ogham marks, my only introduction to writing. Later, Mel taught me Latin letters. "Writing is important, Brigid. You must be literate if you are to communicate with bishops across Europe."

"I don't want to communicate with the bishops," I'd argued. "That's your job. Or Mariah's. Or Conleth's."

"I need your help, Brigid. All the orders for the women, for the nuns. You know Mariah is not suited, nor does she want that kind of leadership. Conleth and I can't keep up with that side of nuns and the monastery too, and well..." he trotted out his ever-present reminder, "...you need them both too."

My head pulsed with an early ache. Druid teachings, histories, and Laws, passed down for generations through word of mouth and patient memorization. Ogham, a druid's series of lines and slashes, was only for simple purposes such as giving directions. Our traditions continued for thousands of years without the need of written word. The Christians, however, found it necessary to put everything in writing. Their teachings, history, and laws were set forever in the Bible.

I found it maddening when Conleth would point to symbols on his scraps of parchment, proclaiming, "This is the Word of the Lord."

"No, it's not," I replied. "Those are symbols copied by your monks."

This letter, which I held, was different from the stories bound into their holy book. It demanded an answer.

I broke the red wax seal and glanced over at the sleeping messenger, still huddled in front of the fire. He had come far to deliver this piece of parchment. My hands shook. I'd received several messages from Britannia in the course of establishing Cill Dara, usually replies to my requests for various inks and robes. Judging by the condition of the exhausted messenger, this letter took priority.

An inquisition, it read, *is being held to investigate the background and behavior of the priest Patrick. We write to you, Abbess, because of your proximity in the wild land of Éire.*

I raised an eyebrow at their description of my homeland.

Information revealed to us, as we deliberated his elevation to Bishop of Éire, encourages us to seek the truth. Monetarily, we are concerned that tithes are being withheld. Additionally, a childhood friend of Patrick's provided us with proof, which substantiates unbecoming rumors, of pagan behaviors during his time enslaved. We ask that you submit to the Tribunal any information pertaining to Patrick that is unbecoming to a Christian man, behavior that may have occurred presently, or in his past.

The missive fell from my hands. Pagan behaviors? What could have happened? Why would they use that against him when all of Éire was raised pagan? What childhood friend? Despite my confrontations and disagreements with Patrick the priest, Patrick the man held my heart. I wouldn't betray him.

Conleth knocked on my door. He held a copy of the same letter.

"What should we do?" he asked. Patrick's visit left Conleth more in awe. "I can't imagine Patrick has any sin, any cause to doubt his appointment to Bishop."

"Then you need to write that to Britannia. Stand up for Patrick if that is what you believe."

"What about you, Brigid? Cill Dara should take the same stance. We could write a letter together to show our unity on this issue." Conleth sat himself comfortably on my bench and pulled me close next to him.

I glanced at my letter again and recalled things I had no right to recall, not now, not next to Conleth.

"Brigid, shall we reply together, write one letter showing Cill Dara's backing for Patrick as Bishop?"

I didn't know how to answer. He took my hand in his, a warm gesture that made me appreciate what a caring man he was.

"I don't know if I can write that letter, Conleth. However, I don't think it is right that someone in Britannia is spreading hurtful rumors about Patrick's past."

"Why couldn't you write the letter of approval with me? Do you not approve of him for Bishop, sanctioned by Britannia?"

"Conleth, you seem to forget I'm not a Christian. The bishops wrote to me because of the title bestowed upon me by Mel years ago. In all honesty, I should not reply to that missive." I leaned my head on his shoulder, comforted by his presence.

"I don't forget," he said as he wrapped his arm around me. "I'm aware of the differences between us, although they don't seem to matter, do they?"

I smiled. "No. I salute the sun each morning, and you say Mass. I care for the sacred flame, and you light prayer candles in your church. Our differences are only on the surface."

He pulled away from me. "I'm not talking about religion. I meant our differences in how we feel about each other."

"I care about you, Conleth, you know that I do." Even as I spoke, I knew it wasn't what he wanted to hear.

"I love you, Brigid, with all that I have. That is not enough for you, is it?"

I shrank from his words. I couldn't explain to him what it was that tied me to Patrick. "Conleth, I'm happy with you, I want to be with you and for us to be together," I said, and meant it.

"No, that's not it." He rubbed his eyes with his hands in exhaustion. "I've wanted more, for some time now. You know this. We've discussed it before." He waited for my reaction. I guessed what he wanted to say, and I couldn't stop him from saying it.

"You know I've wanted marriage and a family, Brigid. I want it with you, even though I know...I know there is something holding you back from loving me completely." I began to protest, but he held up his hand. "Please, Brigid, once again, consider an offer of marriage from me. I will give you the time you need, until Beltane, and I ask that you answer me fully and finally then. Finally."

He emphasized his last word. He wouldn't offer again. I couldn't think of it now when a letter with Patrick's name rested in my hand. "I will answer with my own letter to the archbishop," he concluded and stood to leave. "You answer only what you think you should."

CHAPTER 31

Brigid and Patrick

Snow fell lightly on the land. We stepped out of roundhouses, druids, monks, and nuns, faces upturned, looking to the gray sky, allowing the white flakes to frost their eyelashes. It wasn't much, a dusting, but it was enough to bring smiles to faces weary of winter. I stood in the doorway of my house. I would have been content, except that I ignored the impulse to take action on the summons from Britannia. I must wait, I reminded myself. Let Conleth answer as he would. This is Patrick's fate, and he must decide what to do. I must wait until this visit is concluded. Patrick visited Cill Dara again.

I watched his processional of his monks and guards approach. I pulled my woolen robe around me, finding the thick hood comforting. I settled back into darkness and let the sides of the hood work as blinders. Patrick returned in the winter for official reasons: more talk of a partnership between the monasteries to throw off the hierarchy, though certainly his true reason to visit was the letter. I was one of the few that had yet to answer, and my letter sent to Britannia could be crucial, according to Mel. Father Anthony waited for my opinion.

Cill Dara was one of the most well-known monasteries in Éire. My letter could cause more problems than it would help. I'd have to explain my druid past. Hide my role here in the present. I hoped Conleth's letter would suffice. The more contact I had with church officials, the riskier my position at Cill Dara became. If they discovered the whole truth of the druid presence, I could be sent away, back to Fotharit, where slavery to Maithghean awaited. Again, my fate and Patrick's were intertwined, one dependent on the other.

My love for Patrick? What of it? Had I not yet given up on this hope made lifetimes ago? I hadn't. I longed to see him. Part of me was thankful for the letter. Conleth awaits your answer, I thought to myself angrily, while you wait for Patrick.

The processional slowed and the chariot, which carried Patrick, stopped in the courtyard. I took a deep breath and remembered who I was. I'm Brigid of Cill Dara and one of the Tuatha dé Danann. An otherworldly calm overtook my girlish apprehension. Patrick should be nervous. He did engage in the pagan arts while in Foclut Forest, under my and Dathi's instruction. I knew his past; I was his past. With a single dispatch, I could ruin his dream of becoming a bishop. If they knew the truth, the bishops could ruin me.

His chariot had developed new luxuries, whitewashed and edged in gold carvings. For a moment, I wondered if what Britannia charged about the tithes was true. Patrick stood tall and noble, his tonsured hair now white. His blue eyes, which could change in a flash from mercy to love to damnation, peered out to me. They were the eyes of a young boy, the lonely shepherd boy, lost and in need of help.

He stepped down and walked with me, scrutinizing the groundwork.

"We are doing well since your visit this past summer," I answered. "Brother Conleth had to pick up food and supplies from Dun Ailenn. When he returns, he can quote you the new admissions for monks and nuns."

Patrick nodded, unable to say the true reason why he came. We walked toward the meeting hall, when Melwyn bounded through the light snow across our path.

"Hello, Father Patrick," she said, remembering him from his last visit.

"Hello, Melwyn," he replied to the child.

"Look!" She held up a basket of acorns, collected from beneath the dusting of snow under the sacred oak. "Acorns are special because they grow into big oak trees." She picked up a handful in her pudgy fingers and deposited them into Patrick's hand. "Plant these at your home," she said.

"Is she druid raised?" He rolled the acorns through his fingers. "I thought the nuns took care of her."

"Melwyn is taught both faiths," I explained. "She may choose which she prefers when she's old enough." Cecelia watched her now. We all alternated days caring for the orphan child.

We continued our walk to the gardens as the snow fell, encapsulating the silence. I pointed out where our patch of potatoes would be, and the trellises, waiting for the beans to overtake them in spring.

"Brigid, I didn't come here to survey your frozen vegetable garden." Patrick took a deep breath. "I need to know what word you received from Britannia. The officials have sent letters to all clerics in Ireland. You must have received one as well." Snow fell between us, blurring my vision. "Whatever this letter says, it has damaged my reputation severely. The words have leaked out to the druids. Messengers tell me that Maithghean, in particular, gloats over my impending demotion. Yet, I've no idea what the thing says and what charges have been brought against me."

"Maithghean? Why should he be concerned with you?" Suddenly I was more concerned about this situation. If Maithghean had an interest, it meant he was plotting something.

"I don't know. I can't figure out the minds of druids, particularly that one. My Fotharit connections tell me he's heard about this and can't wait to share what he knows with the bishops. Seeing as how he can't write a letter...I suppose I'm saved. At least for now."

I pulled the folded letter from my pocket. I'd kept it with me since its receipt, not trusting any druid, nun, or messenger who might frequent near my desk. I handed it to him and turned away to contemplate why Maithghean should be involved in this. He knew the truth, or what he thought was the truth. Even if he could find someone to write the letter for him, the bishops would have a hard time believing a random druid.

Patrick's face was impassive as he read. When he finished, he threw it to the ground. "It says nothing. All I know is the words of an old friend suddenly changed the Arch Bishop's mind."

"What words might they have been? What would this friend say about you?" I asked. I picked up the vellum before it became damp, the ink ruined from the snow.

"I can't imagine. I don't even know who..." He looked at me as though he'd never seen me before. His eyes closed and he rubbed his palm across his forehead. "Brigid, I must go to my quarters now. I need to rest and pray about this."

Patrick and Conleth met privately for two days, as the snow fell harder and drifted along the pathways. The two men discussed how to answer the Church's call. Both believed the Irish church to be independent of the British. Yet, at this point, only the Pope in Rome could bestow autonomy to them. It was not Patrick's plan to break from Rome, only to remove the extra step of reporting to Britannia first. Now, this entire plan was in peril, as rumors and allegations swirled around Patrick's name. It was politics by Father Anthony and the British leaders.

"I've written my letter of support," Conleth explained to the man he so admired during our evening meal in the feasting lodge. "I've explained that all of your tithes and collections have returned to the churches here in Éire."

I held my tongue when I overheard this bit of conversation. Patrick didn't give money to Cill Dara. We drew initiates from Armagh, a fact Patrick and his followers in the north didn't appreciate. However, he did help Conleth and Mel at the beginning, before he knew of my presence here. Patrick listened to Conleth's words, but his eyes traveled to Conleth's hand joined with mine discreetly under the table. His face reddened and our eyes caught as Conleth spoke. I pulled my hand away.

"The question is not whether Brigid should write a letter of support," Conleth continued, unaware of the interchange. "Our goal should be to discover who it is that ruins your name in Britannia."

Patrick and I reached for the pitcher of cider at the same time, our fingers touching. A lightning bolt spread through me. Patrick rubbed his fingers, feeling the effects too, while I took the ceramic pitcher and refilled both our mugs.

"I have an idea who is fueling those rumors, Conleth." Patrick continued the conversation. "I believe it is an old so-called friend, Linus, to whom I admitted many things when I returned from my time in slavery." He glanced at me.

What things had he admitted to Linus? With a glimmer of intuition, I understood. He had told Linus about me.

"Well, then, Patrick," Conleth said. "Problem solved. We find your so-called friend, and ask him to recant his silly rumor. What words has he spread around the bishops' council anyhow?"

"His words are of no consequence. It doesn't matter if he exaggerates stories of my past."

"Excuse me." Conleth reached for my hand as I left the table, and I felt Patrick's gaze burn through me.

"His eyes follow you everywhere." Dar ran to catch up with me as I headed toward my home.

"Who?" I asked, not sure to which man she was referring.

"Patrick," she answered. "Brigid, wait. He still affects you, even after all these years, doesn't he?" She linked her arm with mine, and I was glad for the comfort of my old friend. We walked to my house. Inside, I stirred the fire in the hearth.

"I hate that I can't change how I feel. I hate what it is doing to Conleth." I cared for Conleth, perhaps loved him, in a way. But, he was not my anam cara.

"Does Conleth know about Patrick?"

"No, he's innocent. I've never mentioned Patrick to him. It would break his heart."

"I'll keep Melwyn for a few days to give you time alone. I know you have Conleth's offer to consider."

"Thank you." I hugged my friend, grateful for her support.

A knock at the door interrupted us. I expected it to be Conleth, checking on why I left the hall, but it was Patrick.

"I will leave now," Dar whispered. She brushed past Patrick. Her translucent blue eyes studied the frown on his face.

"Why are you here?" I stayed in the doorway so that Patrick remained outside, breaking all the rules of good hospitality.

"I've thought of closing Cill Dara," he said, as if he spoke of how many wheels of cheese we had stored for the winter.

I stared up at the man, baffled.

"If my appointment for bishop is stalled any further, I may consider it."

"Why?" I asked, although I knew why. A powerful move from him might convince the bishops that he was influential enough to join their rank. It would show the strength of his leadership, even as he tried to free himself from their influence. Patrick, the Bishop of Éire.

"This is a pagan sanctuary, Brigid. It is obvious you are using Church funds to run a druid school."

I sighed. "How many times do we have to have this conversation? Mel agreed to the terms that both faiths would be housed here. No Church funds are used for druid study. You may review my accounts if you wish." My frustration with him grew, as snow dusted our hair and shoulders.

"Yet, the money is used for housing and meals that support the druid community, correct? Your abode is as fine as Conleth's." He looked around me, well aware I was breaking hospitality.

I began to panic. "Perhaps when we first began, funds were shared for basic survival. The druid community didn't ask for it."

Patrick stared at the ground, as I explained how this house, because of low druid numbers, became my own. Slowly, my panic started to subside, and I recognized the purpose of his visit, how he had the same frown on his face when he saw Conleth reach for my hand.

"This is not about church money, is it Patrick? Nor is it about your desire for promotion to Bishop. This is about my relationship with Conleth. You want to report me to the church leadership because you are jealous?"

"I remember." He gripped the sharp straw that lined the thatched doorway. I wanted to touch him again then, as I always did, when he mentioned our time together, but I didn't. I steeled myself instead. "You came to me speaking incessantly of pagan gods and goddesses., telling me you were a goddess. Trying to convince me I was some kind of demi-god. You keep me from being Bishop. Because of you, I could lose everything."

"Really?" I asked. "How do you explain that summer, Patrick? Perhaps Linus will explain for you. I don't keep you from your goal. Linus does. Your own drunken stories to him. Will you tell the Pope the goddess you met in order to prove your case against me and Cill Dara? Will you tell the Pope you are the embodiment of an Ancient One?"

The air cracked and tingled between us. Speechless, he seemed to struggle to find words, taken aback at the depth of my anger.

"You listened to me," I continued relentlessly. I would not let him blame me. "You listened and responded. Don't forget our dreams. We are still bound together, whether you like it or not."

"Dreams! The Pope is not going to believe evidence of dreams!"

"What led you here in the first place? Your dream. Our dream, together. We would be victorious, right? You heard me in a dream and ran from your seminary back here. Without permission from the Church. The threat of my letter to Britannia was real. I could write it, if I chose, and support all of Linus's claim s.Whispers echoed off the walls, and Patrick waited in the snowy cold.

"Please," I tried one last time. "If Cill Dara closes, I'll have nowhere to go. My father has sold me to Maithghean. I would return to Fotharit as Maithghean's servant. You know we do this,ultimately, for my protection."

"I didn't realize..." He paused and closed his eyes. I think he thought about me for a change, and not himself and his ambition. My hand met his, both poised on the side of the door. He touched my fingertips gently.

"You can't close this monastery over petty jealousy." Conscious of his touch, I remained still in the doorway but didn't remove my hand. "We may have our differences, and you may hate me for being here, but please, if for no other reason, don't let me become Maithghean's slave."

He looked at me, his blue eyes full of longing.

"I don't hate you. I couldn't return you to slavery," he sighed. "Especially to Maithghean. I'm sorry, Brigid. I'm so sorry I caused this." He brought his hand to my face, framed it in his palm, traced my lips with his thumb. I closed my eyes and wished we could contain this moment forever. Moments passed. I stepped back to allow him into the house. "Come inside with me," I whispered.

"I have to go." His voice cracked as he disappeared into the cold night air.

He slept fitfully in the unfamiliar bed, as he always did when he traveled. Patrick was the lone recipient of a private room in a small beehive shelter, while his monks bunked with the men of Cill Dara. Images of Brigid flashed through his mind and kept him awake.

He still couldn't believe it. The druid woman, the goddess of his youth, was now an abbess, a bishop, but still druid. He wasn't against female clergy, but she had his title. Everyone knew Mel was so drunk he read the wrong rites at what should have been a simple prayer of thanksgiving. Brother Ailbe had begun a movement to strip her of the title, but he didn't get far. The people around Unisech loved Brigid for her charity. Even those in the lands far to the south knew of Brigid's healing abilities and refused to say a bad word against her. So, Brother Ailbe dropped the inquiry, not worth the effort.

Patrick closed his eyes again, this time in prayer. *Dear Lord, please cleanse me of my feelings of envy, a great sin in your eyes. I'm blessed in many ways, enriched by Your love and guidance, and I need not worry about titles and bishops.*

He stopped as his heart tightened. He was not envious of her title, a small voice in the back of his mind reminded him. He was envious of Conleth.

He was pulled into dreams again.

He ran his hands across her body, needing, wanting. He couldn't get enough of her smooth flesh, her breasts heavy in his hands. With his mouth, he traced her form, the hills and curves smelling of sweet clover that he had loved for so long. She moaned beneath him, a sound that spurred him on to further exploration.

"Padraic? Patrick?" she whispered in a flicker of recognition. He smiled, glad that she knew. Her hands, too, caressed him, each touch the exquisite spiral of fire he remembered so well. Never had he felt so whole, so intact, or so certain of where he was meant to be. He buried his face into her coppery hair, his lips pressed against her silky neck, wishing the miraculous minutes that melded them together would last an eternity.

CHAPTER 32

Brigid

When darkness fell, Conleth came to me. "I had to see you." He took me into his arms without delay. His intensity and presence surprised me. He had always been a gentle, tentative lover, as if he were afraid I would break in our moments alone. Not now. He was different. He held me tight and pushed me toward my bed.

"Conleth, why are you here when there are visitors?" We had an unspoken agreement not to meet when church officials were present, in an attempt to make our relationship as tactful as possible. Patrick and his monks were scattered in extra beds and roundhouses across the men's side of the campus. I didn't understand why he came now, when we housed important guests.

"They don't matter." His brown eyes radiated amber, fire, and seared into mine. He kissed me with a fervency that was not his. Something else took him over and somewhere, inside me, I recognized it. This was not Conleth's need. Conleth was moved by something else, someone else. *Patrick.* I knew and I acquiesced. He pulled me to the bed and held me beneath him. Yielding to his strength, I gave myself over to the same commanding tide that carried him.

Conleth rested on my shoulder, breathing heavy as our passion abated. He held me, and I began to close my eyes, allowing the world to go in and out of focus. His arms held me, a builder's arms, thick and strong from years of physical labor. He smelled of stone and timber, from church-building. I studied his rough, squared hands, and identified where a blood blister formed under one fingernail. The hands that caressed me moments ago, I realized, were older, angular, yet still strong. The body next to me had been taller, thinner. Patrick? My body cried out with a surety it remembered. A sinking feeling filled me as Conleth turned away.

He sat up at the edge of the bed, his back toward me.

"Brigid?" he whispered.

"Yes, love?" I answered and touched his back. He lurched aside as if burned.

"How did I get here?" He leaned forward, his head cradled in his hands, and he heaved silent sobs.

"What do you mean?" I moved behind him, encircling him in my arms, but he didn't turn to me.

His tears fell on my hands which rested on his chest, and I clutched him tighter, trying to face him, unable to comprehend the confusion welling up inside him. Several times, he began to speak, his mouth opened and closed, but no words came out.

"Conleth?" I knelt in front of him, wrapping a gray wool throw from the bedcovers around our naked bodies.

"It wasn't me Brigid, it wasn't." He cried even harder. "It was like the time with the warrior and the oak staff. Something else came over me. Someone?" His last word was a terrifying question. I drew back, slowly recognizing the pieces that fit together.

"I wouldn't come here with guests present, you know that. Not with Patrick here, of all people. I was watching the entire time. I saw myself leave my room. I ran here. The need to see you was tremendous. I couldn't stop myself, or whatever..." He broke off, gulping great breaths of air.

"Conleth, you are here now," I tried to hold his hand, to comfort him, but it was no use. He drew away. "You are with me now."

"Brigid, I didn't make love to you. That was not me, yet I watched it all from over there." He pointed to a bench on the far side of the room.

"Conleth, of course it was you. How could it not be?" I said the words but fought a rising tide of panic. I knew the truth. Exactly what happened. He lifted his discarded robe from the floor and dressed quickly. He looked down on me as I sat on the cold floor.

"You didn't say my name," he whispered, his eyes rimmed with red. "I heard you, from over there." He signaled to the bench again.

"No, Conleth. No. You must be mistaken." I wrapped the wool tighter around me. "There is something happening with you…" I reached my hand toward him as the room whirled around me in utter chaos. Conleth opened the door and turned to me before he left.

"You said a name I'd never heard. Padraic, maybe? The old Irish. Then, you spoke the name 'Patrick,' Brigid. I heard you."

"No…" I fought back the sickness that rose within me. I ran to him at the door. This had happened, but how? Patrick had been here, somehow. I couldn't admit it, I couldn't explain it. Not at Conleth's expense. "No, Conleth. Don't leave."

"I'm surprised I didn't see it before. I feel a little stupid, Brigid. I should have noticed the way you act around Patrick. Your insistence on visiting Armagh alone." He shook his head as if to clear away the images. "I know Patrick is the man who holds your heart, not me."

"You must leave Cill Dara. Now." I spoke through gritted teeth, as I flung open the door of the chapel. Patrick rose from his knees where he had been praying.

"Why? Conleth and I are meeting again, to coordinate the flow of new converts into Armagh and Cill Dara. Both monasteries will benefit." He looked sincerely puzzled. "Brigid, what's wrong?"

"Why?" I sneered as I echoed his words. "Where were you last night?" I strode toward him, my fists clenched with a barely controlled rage.

"I was in the guest lodge," he whispered. Then his face reddened. I glared at him.

"I-I-was sleeping," he stuttered. "I didn't leave my room." He stepped aside, so he didn't have to face me, and walked to the window and stared at the snow-covered landscape.

"Your body didn't leave your room, but part of you did, Patrick. *Padraic*." He flinched when I said the second name. He knew it. He recognized it. And he had the power and magic that went with it. "How did you do it? When did you gain this power? Have you had it all along? Did you hide it from me and Dathi all those years ago?" I demanded.

He spun around and gripped my arms. "I didn't use anybody. I had a dream. That is all. You know what my dreams are, but I used no one."

"Last night was not my doing. None of our dreams has been anything I can control now. Those days are past, Patrick. You have a power that you will not admit. But you used it anyway. And you used Conleth, of all people!"

Patrick still gripped my arms, but shook his head. A low "no" emanated from his lips, and his face went white.

"Conleth looks up to you," I said. "He considers you a friend, a mentor. Are you so jealous you must destroy him?" Tears streamed down my face. "I care for him. He doesn't deserve this." Conleth was a good, guileless man, ruined by forces over which he had no control. "Now, he refuses to leave his room, he refuses food and water. He is fasting to try to exorcise demons from his soul," I finished, overwhelmed by guilt.

"I only dreamed, Brigid. I swear to you, I didn't do anything intentional. I've never been able to control the times when we meet in our dreams. Never." He loosened his grip on my arms and sat on a pew. I sat beside him, wiping away my tears.

"Your dream. Last night. You made love to me, didn't you?" I asked quietly. "You used an innocent man to take what you deny yourself."

Patrick stared blankly at the altar. He kept silent.

"Depart Cill Dara in an hour's time," I said. "I expect to find you and your monks gone, or I will go to the Britons with the truth."

CHAPTER 33

Brigid

The weeks following Patrick's departure left me at a loss. I was furious for what he'd done. Yet, part of me was astonished. He had Danann power. He could command someone else to do his bidding. Beyond shape shifting to an element of the earth. According to him it was uncontrolled. Impulsive. But he could do it. He could, with me, bring the Danann back to the world. He could, but he wouldn't.

I was also at a loss with how to apologize and explain to Conleth. I wanted to erase the hurt from him, take back what happened. Conleth refused to speak to me. He avoided the main lodge for meals or any rituals where druid and Christian might both be present. Everyone noticed the tensions between us.

Dar brought Melwyn back to my home, and I was glad for the distraction provided by the little girl.

"I thought Melwyn could spend a few days with you," she said, as she roused me from my bench by the fire.

"Thank you, Dar."

Even though the main injury was Patrick's responsibility, I did keep the truth from Conleth. That guilt weighed on me. "I could have told him about Patrick," I said to Dar.

"I suppose. When? How? What exactly would you have said?"

I didn't know. There wasn't an answer.

"Cecilia and I will be traveling to Dun Ailenn, to consult with Ean. Will you be alright?" Dar was concerned, and she would have canceled her trip if I asked her.

"I'll be fine. Melwyn will help cheer me up." Guiltily, I considered that it was not me that needed the cheering, but Conleth.

"Brigid, you can't wallow like this. You aren't responsible for Conleth's feelings."

"I am responsible, Dar. I brought Patrick here. I kept the truth about my past from Conleth."

"Would Conleth have understood if you tried to explain it?" She sat with me by the fire, as Melwyn arranged her blankets on her sleeping roll. Past lives, gods and goddesses, banished Danann and wandering souls. No, I doubted the practical and pragmatic Conleth would have understood.

"Patrick chose to come here. You told Conleth from the start how you felt, didn't you? He knew you didn't feel the same."

I nodded. I told Conleth another held my heart more than once.

"It was horrible the way it happened for Conleth," Dar continued. "It's not your fault, nor is it Patrick's. You told me he didn't intentionally do these things. He has a power he can't control. They are mysteries, which can't be explained."

"But I knew, Dar. I knew it was not Conleth with me."

She rose to leave and took me into her arms. My friend held me close before she left on her journey to Dun Ailenn.

It was a delight to have Melwyn back. A carefree and loving little girl, she brightened up every day with her presence. If she found me staring off into the fire, she tugged at my sleeve, enticing me to chase her into the fields to pick early spring flowers or play with the skittish lambs.

"Will I be able to wear a blue robe like yours when I grow up, Brigid?" she asked one afternoon as we kneaded dough for our bread.

"You may, if you choose," I replied. "Dar and I wear the robes of the druids. We dedicate our lives to the earth and to the gods and goddesses of Éire."

She punched her tiny fist into the sticky dough. "Mariah asked if I wanted to be a Christian, like her. She gave me these." Melwyn reached into her neckline, smearing dough across her face, and pulled out a rosary made of wood.

"Those are very nice beads, Melwyn."

"Mariah said Christians wear this cross." She held up the wooden crucifix at the center of the rosary, approximately the size of the child's hand. "What do druids wear?"

"Some druids wear necklaces of gold, or maybe bracelets. It depends on their rank and years of study," I explained. I wiped the girl's hands and face with a damp rag.

"What is their sign?" she pressed. "Mariah said the cross is the sign for Christians."

"Ah, the druid symbol you mean?" I paused, knowing there was not a simple explanation, as there was with a cross. "Well, druids usually look outside, at an oak tree, like our Sacred Oak. Or we look at the sun or the stars, or the crops growing in the fields. We understand that life is an unbroken cycle. Just as wheat will die in the fields in the winter, we know it is reborn in the spring."

"What is their picture?" Melwyn asked, finding this topic very important.

"Well, I suppose it could be many things. Most often, it is circles or spirals carved into holy places, sacred stones. They show the unbroken circle of life, death, and life again."

"Can I wear it like this?"

I thought of the old Danann spirals, carved into boulders of power. "We could have the metalsmith make you a spiral. But for now, there is something we can do. Come with me." I led Melwyn outside, pointing out the green grass and buds on the oak trees. Spring was a magical time of rebirth.

"During this time of the year, we pay attention to the sun that will help our crops, and the grass to grow, so the cows and sheep will have food. Lugh is one of the gods who represents the sun."

"Represents?" Melwyn stumbled over the word, as she squinted up to the sky.

"Represents. Lugh is a friend of the sun. Here, we will make our own sun, and that can be your druid sign until we get a necklace made for you."

We sat down in the pasture and picked long stems of grass. I twisted the grass into a knot, working it around the center, weaving the knot outwards. The little girl copied my movements.

"It looks like the sunshine!" She danced happily with her green sun made of grass, a little ragged around the edges. I had a sudden memory of myself as a child in the pastures of Fotharit with Father. A sharp pang went through me. I missed my father. Rather, I missed who he had been, before Maithghean's darkness influenced him.

"Brigid, it looks a little bit like a cross." Melwyn held her weaving next to her rosary at her neck.

"I suppose it does, just a little bit," I marveled at the insights a child could bring.

CHAPTER 34

Brigid

"Brigid." A man's desperate whisper drew me from sleep. I fumbled in the night for a candle and spark on the table next to my bed.

"Brigid." The voice rose. Patrick. I threw the flint stone aside and trusted the banked embers of my fireplace to lead me to the door. I opened it, and Patrick entered in a cold rush, chills emanating from his robes.

He threw his arms around me, face wet with tears. "Please, Brigid," he begged. "Hide me. They are coming to take me to Britannia. I can't go." His breath came in rapid bursts, and I was afraid he would faint.

"Patrick, calm down. What's going on?" I led him by the hand into the sitting room and rekindled the fire in the hearth while he spoke.

"You know Linus has told all to the bishops?" He began. "The Bishop of Britannia contacted me himself. They accuse me of stealing tithes. Even more, they are using Linus's assertion that I'm a pagan idolater. He sent so-called messengers supposedly to assure my safe passage over the sea so I may testify before the Tribunal. If they take me, they will not allow me to return to Éire. They will put me in prison."

An interrogation before the bishops' council usually meant dismissal. Mel told me his share of gossipy stories. Patrick worked for years to be ordained bishop, and his life's goal balanced on a very thin line. The Church distrusted him, believing he took tithes for his own use. Linus's rumors were just that: he could prove nothing about an enslaved young man imagining a goddess, or imagining being a god, but the rumors were powerful enough to add fuel to the flames of condemnation.

A pre-dawn light filtered in through the narrow window, and I saw fully the disheveled man sitting before me. No longer was he the charismatic priest, surrounded by adoring followers and loyal monks. His robe was dirty, and he looked like he'd burrowed into a hay wagon. The hem was worn and frayed. He had walked for miles. Alone. He was now a scared man with nowhere else to turn.

"How did you manage to travel here?" I inquired. The bishops' messengers were most likely guards, ordered not to let Patrick out of their sight.

"I escaped." A wry smile played on his lips when he saw my questioning glance. "Brigid, you know I'm perfectly able to slip past guards...although my skills were a bit rusty." Patrick's hands shook. "I will not return to Britannia, but I will write a letter in my defense instead. Linus's claims will not go unnoted."

I brought him unfinished bread from my previous night's meal. I set the water to heat and added calming chamomile petals in to seep while he told the story of sneaking out of his own monastery. He gnawed at the bread loaf. "You're the only one I can turn to, Brigid." His words bewildered me.

"Why did you come here?"

"Cill Dara is my refuge." His blue eyes were honest and scared. "Brigid, you are my refuge."

Did he want the shelter of my sanctuary, a place he threatened to close not long ago, or did he want me? My protection? Or the protection of Brigid, the goddess?

Patrick visibly swallowed at my silence, as though he just realized I could refuse him shelter and send him straight to the bishop. He groped for words to fill the space. "Brigid, you are the only person on this earth who truly knows me. You know why I can't return to Britannia. I need time to respond to the Tribunal and to send my response through a messenger."

"Is that all?" I asked bitterly. I had made many allowances for him. Losing Conleth hurt. "You're putting my position and my school in great jeopardy. I've worked to make Cill Dara succeed. I've compromised my own beliefs. I've lost my home and family because of it. You threatened to close the place where you now beg for shelter. You broke my relationship with Conleth."

He dropped his last bit of bread, blue eyes wide, like a frightened child, despite the white streaks in his hair. The look in my eye told him I was serious. I could do more than refuse him shelter. Heat rose to my brow and crowned my head with a goddess's golden glow. I could notify not just Britannia and the bishops, but Rome and the Pope. I could corroborate my story with Linus. I had the power to ruin Patrick of Éire forever.

"Brigid, you said you would help me," Patrick whispered.

Power, dormant for so long, filled me. Cill Dara, the school of the oak, was my domain. Energy rushed from beneath my feet and through my body. The Ancient pulse began. "You said you would help me," I said in an otherworldly voice. Brigid. The Danann Goddess. Sister of Fodla. Daughter of Macha. The Ancient Ones. The Goddess who escaped the underground.

He saw the change that flowed through me. "Perhaps...perhaps...I've spoken harshly in the past. I should not have done so."

"Do you take back your words, then? Your threats to close this school, the last place where druids can learn the ancient ways?"

Patrick sat still as I paced across the room. Something else controlled me. Someone else. As if all of the Danann combined into one.

Finally, he answered. "Cill Dara is a refuge. It is a holy place, blessed by the Church." He chose his words carefully. He didn't meet my eye.

"You answer what is safe. You don't say what you believe." I absorbed strength from each individual sunbeam. *Thank you, Lugh.*

"I know too much, Brigid. What you know of my past, I know of yours. It is difficult for me to unite my knowledge of you then ...and you now." His shoulders wilted.

"You don't need to unite that knowledge, because I am the same," I said. "Brigid of the past, *Bride*. Brigid of your youth. Brigid of now. It is me, *Padraic*. It has always been me."

Heat streamed through my fingertips and rose through the soles of my feet, which illuminated my robe. I drew strength from the brightness. Patrick raised his eyes to meet mine, he, too, encircled in the light.

Locked in the sacred space, we studied each other's souls. He was frightened at first, until he saw. Inside the light filled sphere, we revealed ourselves. He saw everything: the past, Padraic, the Danann, the battles...other lives, together always.

"Do you understand that all Gods are One?"

"I understand," he replied. "It is not the path I chose. I serve the Lord Jesus, not a chief druid, nor the Danann people."

I saw the purity of belief in his spirit. However much I longed for the past, it wasn't now. It wasn't our present lives. "Nor do I serve the titles of Danann or druid or bishop," I said. "I serve Éire. I only ask you to do the same."

He nodded in acceptance. The light receded. We returned to ourselves and it was me, in my nightgown, barefoot.

"You may stay here, Patrick. Cill Dara will provide you refuge."

CHAPTER 35

Brigid

Patrick hid in the lower recesses of the granary. Storage existed there, rough stone spaces hewed into the earth. It was barely room enough for a tall man and his bedding. I gave him vellum and ink from my own supply, knowing the cost of the expensive materials. I closed the area off, ostensibly due to a mouse infestation. It would be unsafe to store our winter supply of grain in such conditions. The granaries and its stores were considered women's work, something Conleth never bothered with. Only I held the key.

Word traveled quickly among the Irish clergy that Patrick had gone missing. In hushed tones, Mel approached me with the news that Patrick's followers were worried, even though he'd given Armagh notice he was traveling on a missionary trip, he'd now been gone for weeks. There were also rumors of British messengers from the Church searching for him.

"When the clerics in Armagh asked, I replied I last saw him traveling along the coast," Mel said, sipping on his wine worriedly. Conleth joined us for the meeting. He sat down in my house stiffly, having not spoken to me for two cycles of the moon. Red hurt was visible between us.

"We all know he was called to the Tribunal in Britannia," Conleth said. "Perhaps he went to fight for his title of bishop."

"He's lived on this island longer than I have," Mel said. "He should be ordained. All of this nonsense about past rumors is ridiculous. I hope he has gone ahead to fight those charges." Mel refilled his cup. "But why would the Britons send messengers here? Did their paths cross?"

"Perhaps." I touched the key in my pocket. "However, we can't let people know about the scandal any more than they already do. We can assume he's in Britannia, but we don't know for sure."

"Why shouldn't people know he's fighting for the title of bishop?" Conleth argued. His tone was sharp, and I flinched when he spoke.

"Because it may not happen. The Church could be calling him out for punishment. They believe he has been stealing tithes."

Conleth shrugged, not concerned about Patrick's reputation. I didn't really believe the excuses I gave Conleth. I had to come up with a plan for time that would save Patrick. "We can't say anything to anyone."

"You're right," Mel said. "We don't want the druids to know there may be a problem. Maithghean, in particular, has demanded a meeting with Patrick. Since he has not been seen or heard from, your kin at Fotharit are prepared to demand his exile from Éire."

"What? Why would Maithghean call for a meeting with Patrick?" Maithghean's animosity toward me was unending. He didn't care about Patrick, but he knew that I did. That he demanded Patrick's exile was no surprise. Why Maithghean demanded a meeting with Patrick concerned me. "Maithghean will not let Dunlang turn Christian."

"Perhaps the words of Christ work in mysterious ways," Bishop Mel said.

I didn't believe that. "No, Mel. Maithghean is planning a trap of some kind. He has no love for Patrick. Between the chief druid and the bishops, Patrick is in serious trouble."

"We must help Patrick," said Mel. "We can hide him here if necessary. If he appears."

I'd told no one Patrick was already here, in hiding, waiting for the British messengers he so feared to go home.

"No!" Conleth spat the word. "Cill Dara will have no part in secrets and lies." He glared at me, and I looked away.

"Well," Bishop Mel glanced at Conleth. "We can't make any decisions about Patrick without Patrick. We will wait for word from him and say nothing more about his disappearance."

"Conleth, can we talk? Please?" I followed him outside after Mel left. He stalked to the river and ignored my pleas. I ran until I caught his arm, and he stood still under the oak tree.

Hurt showed starkly in his eyes. "You may not love me, Brigid," he ground out the words through clenched teeth. "I know you don't. Please, don't allow him protection here."

I turned away to face the rushing river. A lie upon a lie. At what point could I tell Conleth the truth? Every answer would hurt him even more. Conleth stood behind me and I sensed his closeness. He began to encircle me with his arms, our old habit at this place. Then he pulled himself back.

"Where will he go, if not here?" I asked.

Conleth made a sharp, strangled sound in his throat. "I don't care, Brigid. I don't care where Patrick goes. The Church has called him back to Britannia. He should go there!" He paced along the river's edge. "They can defrock him permanently or send him to Rome and make him the Pope. I only want him away from you." His voice broke.

I leaned against the trunk of the oak tree. I didn't want to be responsible for another betrayal. "Conleth," I stopped. I had no words, none I had not spoken already. I couldn't tell him. He was so angry right now he would go straight to Britannia. I loved Patrick, rightly or wrongly, and chose Patrick over him, even if Patrick didn't choose me in return.

"I don't want to lose you." My words were weak, but true. I met him at the river's edge and looked him in the eye. "I don't want to lose what we had."

"Ah, so you would like me and Patrick? Both? Oh, rare, that." Acid filled his voice. His brown eyes started with tears, like a small boy's, looking for any sign of hope. I could give him none.

CHAPTER 36

Brigid

Word that Maithghean wanted to meet with Patrick concerned me more than the Church searching for him. "You mustn't go to him," I warned as I unlocked the heavy door to the stone walled cellar and handed him clean robes from the monks storage.

"To whom?" Patrick asked, uncertain of my dire message.

"Maithghean. He has called for you to meet with him, and under no circumstances can you do that." I pushed the door open, allowing cool spring air to filter into the damp cellar. Patrick stood, obviously grateful for the opportunity to stretch his long legs. He stayed hidden during the day, writing his letter to the bishops, and I met him well after midnight so he could walk freely down to the river.

"I can't go anytime soon. I had no intention of meeting with Maithghean, until this situation with the Britons was cleared up anyway," he said.

The river was Patrick's favorite place to spend his freedom in the dark nights. I didn't need to go with him. Often I didn't, but this time I followed him as he sat where Conleth and I used to meet.

"I don't mean now." I joined him on the flat rock. "I mean never. You must never go to Maithghean."

"Why not?" He dipped his hand into the water and allowed it to trickle through his fingers. "I visited before without harm even though I know you have personal reasons for disliking the man."

"It's not just my dislike of him, or the fact that I am, by law, his slave." Chills struck me as I thought of the narrow thread of my fate. "Maithghean is manipulative. He has found a reason to use you, for something. That is his only motivation for requesting your attendance."

Patrick smiled at me, the moonlight reflected upon his face. "Perhaps he requires a Christian to hear his repentance of evil and acceptance of Christ." His tone was sarcastic but I guessed part of him wished it were true.

"Patrick, listen to me. Maithghean has no intention of converting. He is using you to get to me, somehow. I haven't discovered his reasons."

"To get to you? He doesn't know of our connection." He shook the water from his hand, splashing cool droplets on us both.

"He does know. Don't you remember? You went to Fotharit looking for me. He's threatened me with his knowledge of you before."

"Threatened you? So what if he knows I went looking for a healer years ago? Or if he knows about our meetings regarding the Church?"

I sighed and wished Patrick were not always so naïve. "No, Patrick. He knows *everything* about us, everything that could ruin you. Our past. All of our pasts. He is eager to find you, because he could corroborate with Linus. Their stories together could ruin you."

"How would he know?

"I think he first discovered it when I was young, before I understood who you were." I swallowed bitterly, recalling what I could about the Test of the Ancients.

"What did you tell him?"

"I told him nothing. Not on purpose. Maithghean is devious. He has a way of figuring things out, even when I was a child. I think he knew about my past before I did." Then I reminded Patrick about the Test of the Ancients, how Maithghean drugged me, took me to the oak grove, and unlocked the memories I didn't know I had. "When the Test was over, he knew about you. I don't know what I said."

He pressed his face into his hands, as if trying to erase the last few minutes of our conversation. We sat by the river, listening to water fall upon rock.

The first faint edges of pink filtered through on the eastern horizon, and the grass sparkled with drops of dew. Patrick watched the few moments of sunrise allowed to him during his self-imposed confinement.

I welcomed the sun to a new day and stretched my arms and spirit in a long-practiced druid greeting. I closed my eyes and performed the motions I learned as a child, lifetimes before, the movement druids used every morning. Raising my arms to the sky, I reached toward the light, and I invited it to flow into me. Silently, I sent my thoughts to Lugh, the one Danann who had not left my side. We shared our power in the fire and the sun.

"That was beautiful," Patrick said.

"It's a greeting, welcoming the sun. A simple prayer, that's all."

He studied me as the sun rose behind me. He touched a few wisps of my hair that brushed against my face.

Our eyes connected in the hushed mist of the morning. The light grew bright and the river sang glints of gold, which reflected off the blue of his gaze.

I love you. No matter what happens, know this. We spoke in the old way, the Ancient way, the silent way.

I know. I love you, too.

We smiled as we heard each other's thoughts in the light of day, not in the nightmare of inexplicable dreams. We climbed up the slick riverbank and hurried to return Patrick to his hideaway. He took a risk when he stayed outside until dawn. Barefoot, I slipped and slid back down toward the river. Patrick laughed like a carefree young man when he saw me covered in mud. He took my hand and pulled me up.

"Come, Brigid," he chuckled. "Now you do look like you've just emerged from the earth, with all the fairies." I grasped his hand, enjoying the spontaneity. I had not seen him laugh in a very long time.

We clambered to the top of the bank, holding hands, erupting in spontaneous spurts of laughter as we skidded like children across the dewy grass. We fell again, soaked now in the dampness of the turf, and Patrick's face was close to my own. Lines etched his face, yet the happy sparks in his blue eyes showed the boy he had once been, the man he had once been, lifetimes ago.

We were unsheltered, in plain view of Cill Dara's tower, not hidden in a space of dreams and magic. He leaned forward and kissed me ever so slowly, like he had only in the secrets of our dreams, years ago in the pasture. Tears stung my eyes, and his too, as the kiss lasted.

He pulled an errant clover from my hair and put the small shamrock into his pocket. We lifted our eyes from each other and walked together again. We crossed the hillside to the grounds of Cill Dara, hands together in the daylight.

"Stay behind the hedge," I whispered as we realized we had spent too long outside. Cill Dara was awake. "After the first Angelus bells, the monks will all be in the chapel, and you can go to the cellar."

"Brigid?" On the apex of the hill, Conleth stood motionless as he absorbed the sight of Patrick and me, hands joined.

"Oh, Conleth, no." My heart wrenched. Conleth must have seen us as soon as we rose from the riverbank. Patrick dropped my hand, but that didn't matter either as we neared Conleth.

"You promised he wouldn't come here." Conleth ignored Patrick and spoke directly to me.

"I promised nothing," I replied. Words were inadequate and wrong. I could say nothing to eradicate the pain he felt, now doubly imposed. "Patrick needed temporary shelter, and I wouldn't deny him that."

"It looks like you have denied him nothing," he hissed with a coldness I didn't know he was capable of.

"Conleth!" Patrick's authoritative voice rang out, and he placed a kind hand on the younger man's shoulder. "You're gravely mistaken. There is nothing shameful between Brigid and myself. Come, brother in Christ, allow me to explain."

Conleth shook off Patrick's hand and glared at his former mentor, unforgiving. "You're no brother of mine, Patrick."

He brushed past us. "Both of you, leave me be. I've no further words for this." Conleth ran down the hill and toward the river, his stifled sobs echoing in our ears.

CHAPTER 37

Brigid

C onleth told no one about Patrick's presence. A few days later, however, he let me know he was leaving. He stopped at the healing lodge with blankets and water bags draped over a sturdy brown nag.

"I'll go to Rome with Father Anthony. They've arranged for a ship to the east of here." Conleth held a satchel of his belongings at his side. Cill Dara rose up behind him, the new village he'd helped to build.

"Conleth, your place is here. Look at all you have created." I set aside the bundle of sage I'd tied together to dry.

"My place isn't here, Brigid. I can't stay knowing someone else is here with you. He is the one who fills your heart." He stared at the road behind me. "My path leads to Rome."

Patrick no longer dared from his cellar. Rumors came to us the following day of British men at Dun Ailenn. If the British messengers found Patrick, they would force him to go to Britannia, and, most likely, he believed, the bishops wouldn't allow him to return to Éire. So, he stayed underground, unable to bid farewell to the man who was once his friend.

"You hid him without my permission or knowledge," Conleth said.. "You didn't need my permission, but out of respect for what we shared, you could have been honest with me."

It would have destroyed him to hear me say I loved Patrick best, I thought. Words I would never dare say aloud to Conleth. He wanted honesty, but he'd touched on the hurt that full honesty would bring. I would grant Patrick anything, even endanger Cill Dara to give him shelter. I clasped Conleth's hand, strong from the work of building this place, a druid and Christian blend. I couldn't bear to think of him going across the waters to Rome. As I held his hand, a wave of uneasiness washed over me. An image, the vision from years before, flashed in my mind: his hands covered in blood. "Conleth, you mustn't go. Please, stay."

He pulled his hand away. "No, Brigid. I already told you I would keep my silence about Patrick if I meet the Britons on the road east. The ship will sail in a few days, and I've a long way to travel to the harbor."

"I'm not asking you to stay for me. I'm worried. The road is dangerous. Take a warrior from Dun Ailenn, or a monk with you, at least." Even that wouldn't push back the foreboding I felt. "Stay, please."

He picked up his satchel and turned to me, bitterness flashing in his eyes. "What will I do instead?" he challenged. "Stay here and wait for a woman who doesn't love me? Watch while you wait for a man who doesn't love you?"

"He does love me." I reached for the sage and twine again, something to keep my hands busy, because I couldn't admit that Conleth spoke the truth.

"Believe what you will, Brigid. You hear me now. I've seen it a thousand times: a man who dangles a woman by a thread, calling on her when it suits his purpose."

"It isn't like that," I said curtly. Never would he understand about Padraic, or the lonely shepherd, or all the lifetimes in between.

"It doesn't matter now." He walked outside and arranged his bag on the old nag. "I do love you, Brigid." He waited, but I couldn't return his words.

"How can you, Conleth," I asked instead, "when you know my soul is tied to Patrick?"

"Penance?" His mouth lifted into a sad grin as he gathered the reins in his hands.

"Can I not convince you to stay? I fear for your safety on this journey." I pressed a a leather pouch of medicinal herbs into his hands. Willowbark, mint, marigold.

He took the bag and tied it to his belt. "Thank you Brigid, but fear for my heart if I stay."

I passed the hours after Conleth's departure in silent emptiness. My friend and lover was gone, though he had been neither in recent months. He knew how I felt all along, I thought in defense, pushing back the guilt. Those thoughts were little comfort as the sun set to the west and the night grew cold.

In his cellar, Patrick waited. I brought him food and drink every morning and night but left quickly. I couldn't stay with him while I sorted through what Conleth said. Was Patrick tormenting me with what we could never have? Not in this life, not in this situation. Why would I risk the school for him? My own safety? I spent hours alone in meditation, working through the unanswered questions.

Three days later, a breathless rider entered our gates, his grand stallion covered in froth. Horses such as this were reserved for the kings in Éire, and I wondered who lent him the magnificent animal.

"I must speak to the Abbess of Cill Dara," the man informed the guards.

"I am she," I answered. I had walked to the entrance when I heard the frantic pound of hoof beats along the road. My heart leapt momentarily, thinking perhaps Conleth returned.

The man squinted as if looking for the Christian cross on my breast, but found the dark blue robe close enough to a nun's garments.

"Your priest." The disheveled man pulled his skin of water from his pouch and took a long swallow. "Conleth was found yesterday dead on the roadside."

He stated it so matter-of-fact, in between gulps of water from his water bag, that I didn't believe him at first.

"What?" I whispered. Mariah and several other nuns, returning from the morning Angelus, saw the visitor at the gate and joined me.

"Wolves. It looks as if wolves attacked him on the road. A wagon comes behind me with his body." The messenger finished his drink and wiped his muddy sleeve across his mouth with a flourish.

The blood drained from my face and bile filled my throat. Conleth, dead? I foresaw danger, but I didn't expect his death. Mariah put her arm around me, and several of the younger nuns began a keening wail that brought monks and druids running to us.

The wagon approached. A shrouded body jolted disgracefully in the back of the wagon, the snowy linen smudged with dust and debris from its travels.

Dar stopped short next to me. "Oh, Brigid." She took my other hand. Mariah choked back a strangled sob at the sight. Blood stained the white linen. The messenger halted the ugly journey and walked to the back of the wagon.

"You need to identify him if you want him buried here," he said without ceremony. "If he's not your man, we'll take him to Dun Ailenn."

He peeled back the covering, revealing Conleth's alabaster face. The movement loosened the shroud and a bloodied hand fell through the opening, a soft thud on the wooden wagon boards. His strong, square hands that built the church, callused from work yet tender when he touched me, were now ruined.

His hand from my vision, years before, the cold, ragged flesh, brown, red, blood-covered. Clairvoyance rarely came to me and, mistakenly, I had assumed the prophecy was fulfilled when I set his broken fingers. Now, the vision was grotesque and real.

"He's ours. It is Brother Conleth," Mariah spoke with the efficiency of a healer who has dealt with corpses as a matter of course. I found no words, only my stomach twisted in sickness, which compounded my sense of loss. The hollow that greeted me when Conleth left was nothing compared to the knowledge of his death, a horrid death.

"Well, then," said the driver of the wagon. "Where should we take him?" I stood frozen to the spot, unable to move, unable to process the scene before me. Dar took over and led the driver to the chapel. Mariah stayed by my side.

"Come, Brigid," she urged, her hand firm on my elbow. "We must prepare the burial herbs for his body." I went with her, my feet dragging like stones.

Mangled and torn, his body had been a feast for a starving wolf. The creature, most likely out of Conleth's line of vision as he rode his mule east, attacked Conleth's right side. He'd tried to fight the wolf with his hands. A deep gash ripped his throat, showing immediate blood loss from the jugular. The beast searched, as all animals do, for the innards, looking for the succulent nourishment of the liver.

Mariah, always the professional, went white as we examined the wounds.

"I've never seen it this bad," the tall nun whispered. "Not even on dying warriors on the battlefield." Perhaps it was the knowledge of how he died: not a victorious soldier armed with a shield, but a peaceful man who began a holy pilgrimage to Rome.

I moved numbly over the body as I tied bandages and stitched gaping flesh, preparations for burial. His damaged hand, broken fingers, and punctured skin from wild incisors lay on the side of the bench. I ignored it.

"May God and Mary watch over his soul," Mariah prayed as we labored.

"God and Mary didn't do a thing," I said. Mariah stopped her work, stunned. Never had I said a word against her religion. I always professed respect for her beliefs. "God and Mary don't care about this good man, they didn't watch over his soul in life. Why should they in death?" My tone was venomous.

Druids believed in reincarnation. Conleth's soul passed on to a new life, reborn perhaps this very day to a warm and waiting family. This I found more comforting than imagining his soul, rootless as it floated through purgatory or to heaven, searching for a god who allowed such a terrible, painful death to happen.

Mariah and I finished our work in silence. I left her with the body and allowed the Christians to bury him however they pleased. The druids would say farewell in our own way.

The key jangled as I fitted it through the rusty lock. Patrick jumped up when he heard me, banging his head on the low ceiling.

"Where have you been?" he asked, his tone somewhere between worried and demanding.

I drew back, ready to snap at him. For the first time in three weeks, I had not brought him his morning meal. I was the only person with the key and the only one who knew he was here. Unless he could bash through the thick oak door with a few stones, he could die in this small dank room, if forgotten by his keeper.

He paused when he saw my face. "Brigid, what's wrong?" He touched my shoulder.

"Conleth." I swallowed hard and set his basket of bread and cheese on his bench. I handed him a mug of tea. "He's gone."

"Well, yes, you told me he was going to Rome..."

"He's dead. He was attacked by wild animals, half a day's journey from here."

Patrick's face blanched. He sat down on the bench, and the bread and tea scattered to the floor.

"Our Father, who art in heaven, hallowed be thy name..." He crossed himself and mumbled prayers to his God above. I watched his Christian ritual with a strange detachment, as he asked his Lord to take Conleth's soul into heaven.

Later, Bishop Mel repeated Patrick's words when he performed the Christian funeral for Conleth. At the far end of the field, a druid's cairn was prepared for him. I spent three days digging a great space for my friend to rest, filling it with his worldly goods: bowls from his kitchen, a set of dyes to make ink for his beautiful artwork, and a tiny charm from Melwyn. The druids surrounded the cairn, while the Christians prepared their own burial beside the church. Mariah and I fought bitterly over this.

"He was a priest, Brigid. He will be buried next to his church."

"He was Irish. He deserves a burial in the manner of his ancestors." There was no giving in from either side. Still, Mariah held the body, and that possession gave us our final answer.

"We will still prepare an Irish burial for him," Dar told me, enraged. She too, was angered at the Christian ownership of a man who provided kindness to all, no matter what their creed.

"Will you please lead the ritual," I begged her. "I can't." Emotionally empty, I couldn't call upon the forces of nature to witness this. It was the spirits of the earth that killed him. This thought stayed with me, sacrilegious as it was. Animals of the earth destroyed Conleth. Why? It wasn't winter. The wolves should have been fat with spring deer.

Dar gathered the druids to the cairn empty of a body.

"It does not matter where his flesh lies," she began. "His spirit of goodness, his soul, has been reborn into another realm."

We all joined hands, and for the first time in days, a faint spark of light coursed through me. We chanted our goddess prayers over and over until the light filled us.

CHAPTER 38

Brigid

I steadied my breathing before the flame and stared into its light as it burned. Every day, I marveled at its survival, and at mine, when Conleth was so terribly taken away. Empty still, was the space left by Conleth's death. Guilt over our relationship and how it ended consumed me. Imaginations of how he died haunted me. At night, I awoke in a cold sweat as yellow wolf eyes chased me through the forest. I struggled to escape their grasp just as Conleth must have struggled to free himself from the wolves' teeth. I floated through my days, unsure of which way to turn.

I focused again on the flame within the cauldron and sank my energies into the earth, grounding with years of practice. A rote exercise.

Frantically, Cecilia called my name. "Brigid, there is a man at the gate asking for you. For you and Patrick." She crouched low beside me, hidden by the hedge.

"For Patrick?" I asked. "Is the man a British messenger? Father Anthony or one of their priests?"

She shook her head. "No, he was hooded, and I sensed a glimmer of magic. Could it be...?" Cecilia left her question unfinished.

Maithghean, I was sure of it. Somehow, he knew Patrick was here. If he arrived cloaked in magic, then he had dangerous plans. I had to think quickly.

"Get Dar and all the druids you can find. Hide Melwyn, get her out of my house. Send a rider to Dun Ailenn and ask that Ean and his druids come here with as much power as they can bring."

"What about their warriors?" Cecilia asked, ready to do as I requested.

"Send them, though swords will do no good with Maithghean. He can only be defeated with magic of equal strength to his own. We will create a protective circle around us, around Cill Dara."

"Brigid, he's already at Cill Dara's gates. A circle of light won't help us now."

"I know, Cecilia. I can think of nothing else. Please get Dar and Ean."

She ran off, and I dashed to the cellar to release Patrick. The last thing he needed was to be cornered by Maithghean in a room with no escape. I hid behind the buildings, for the first time thankful for their stony strength and solidity.

Cecilia's warning reached the monks as well. The usually peaceful men were gathering tools and pitchforks to protect their stake from the evil stranger. I caught a glimpse of the hooded man as I ducked into the cellar of the granary. He must have overcome the guards with a spell.

I found Patrick surrounded by wasted pieces of vellum. The parchment was expensive, and it was on the tip of my tongue to rebuke him.

"Brigid, why are you here so early?" He was worn, haggard from hours of writing. The task was as laborious for him as it was for me.

"There's no time, Patrick. Maithghean has stolen in through our gates. We have to leave." I pulled him by his hand, but he refused to budge.

"Maithghean?" he questioned. "Can't we talk to him?"

"Patrick, I told you before, he's not to be trusted at all, not ever. He is here to take me away, and to harm you."

"He can't take you from Cill Dara, not while you're on Church land." He turned back to his letter and scratched his quill through another line of unknown text.

"No, Patrick!" I begged, and then he was there. Maithghean was covered in a black robe and hood. Absolute fear froze me where I stood, and even Patrick was silenced at the sight.

"I've come for what is mine," the old man hissed. "Brigid, you are wanted in Fotharit." Maithghean's eyes and teeth were more yellow than I'd ever seen; his face more wizened. Yet, he walked with a straight spine. He was still strong.

Patrick stepped in front of me as a protective shield. "She won't return. No more druid threats."

"Don't call him a druid," I hissed in return. "He doesn't represent me or any other druid."

"Come with me, Brigid. Your father misses you." Maithghean reached a gnarled hand toward me. Both Patrick and I shrank back toward the wall in disgust. There was no window in Patrick's cellar and only the one door Maithghean blocked. I tried to think of some way we could blend with the walls, use the ancient Danann arts to move past Maithghean.

"You can't escape," said Maitghean as if he knew my thoughts. "Brigid, you and I will leave together. Patrick will allow you to leave, unless he wants to meet the same fate as your other priest."

"What other priest?" Patrick gripped my hand tightly in his. "Conleth?"

"What did you do to Conleth?" I asked, feeling sick. The corners of Maithghean's mouth turned up into a smile. The yellow teeth. The yellow eyes.

"I called the wolves," Maithghean said. A cold chill permeated my blood. Maithghean did have the abilities to control small animals, usually to calm them before a sacrifice. Wolf attacks on humans were rare. "I became one of the wolves."

Became? Was he able to shape shift into an animal. If Patrick could inhabit Conleth to do his will, did Maithghean have the power to do the same with the wolves? I wrapped my hand around the small dagger I kept in my pocket. Patrick slammed his fist into the old man's face before I could use my knife.

Maithghean crumpled to the floor. I knelt beside him, prepared to slit his throat. Patrick pulled me away.

"Don't kill him, Brigid. Don't fall into his evil. Get the guards and have this mess removed." Patrick stepped over the body. Energy surrounded Maithghean. I understood what the magician was doing. He wasn't injured. Energy pulled into him and pulled us toward him, like a magnet.

"He's gathering strength from the elements. Run!"

Maithghean rose, tall and terrible. It was not even his face. Instead, a moving mass of anger and hatred, stored from one lifetime to the next.

We slammed the door to the cellar behind us. The heavy oak door did little good. The thing followed us, propelled by anger. I couldn't reconcile the depths of power Maithghean possessed. Patrick pulled me with him, and we ran while I spoke words and charms to deflect what evil I could, if only to slow Maithghean briefly.

"Where should we go?" Patrick and I raced across the grounds. It was all happening too fast. We had no time to plan for an encounter such as this. The protective circle formed by the druids, if it worked, would serve to keep Maithghean in. I couldn't let him hurt anyone else here. He only wanted us.

"To the woods. We must lead him out of Cill Dara," I said. Perhaps it would give Ean and the other druids from Dun Ailenn a chance to arrive and protect what they could.

We crashed into the darkness, surrounded by a forest of oak and hazel. I knew the paths well from gathering herbs and medicines in the daylight. Now the sun had set, and we ran deeper.

"What about the wolves?" Patrick spoke my same thought. Maithghean could try to kill from a distance. Painfully, we both thought of Conleth, an innocent man caught in our entangled lives.

"I don't think he wants us dead. He wants me alive, to return to Fotharit as his slave." I didn't add that Maithghean had no motivation to keep Patrick alive. He would kill him just to hurt me.

"Why, Brigid? You haven't returned there for many years. Why does he still want you? He could buy a slave anytime."

I led him to a large hollow of an old oak. It was barely enough room for the both of us. We crawled in to rest.

"We can reach our thoughts and energy to the Danann. They will help if they can."

"Prayers to God and Christ can save us as well," Patrick replied.

We closed our eyes. He clutched his rosary bead; a small click sounded as he passed each one. I listened to the earth, to the wind and the trees. The forest was eerily still, as if we all held our breath in anticipation.

In desperation, I tried to reach the Tuatha dé Danann. Macha, Dagda, Eiru. They had been silent since I aligned with the Christians, and now I needed their help, as they once needed mine. I needed Lugh to help fill me with light, yet darkness surrounded us. I sank into the tree, reaching like the roots of the oak, in the earth below.

"Please, Dagda, help us." I called to my father from lifetimes ago. He owed me nothing. Below us, they stirred. Good. They heard. They listened. There were small murmurings of conversation, of awakening.

The man who was to be your voice risks death. Padraic.

Padraic is in danger, I told them, *as am I.*

Bres works to defeat us all.

Bres?

Why did the Danann warn me about Bres? We waited, cramped in the hollow of the oak. Patrick was too tall to stay much longer. Ancient sacrifices were once made here, I realized, with a shiver of foreboding. Prisoners, forced into the inner recesses of the oak, which gave life, died here for their sins. Patrick continued his whispered prayers.

Get out! A voice called on the wind. Macha. She gave me a warning.

Patrick looked at me. He heard it too.

"Maithghean will find us." I clutched a handful of acorns in my palm. I collected whatever elements I could, depositing bits of magic into the pocket of my skirt.

"We should go back to Cill Dara," Patrick replied. "There is more protection for us there."

If Dar and Ean's power worked, the school would be protected by light energy. We had drawn Maithghean away long enough for them to accomplish their task. I was surprised Patrick knew this.

"There's another path to the north of us. It's a long way back to the grounds, but perhaps one Maithghean does not know about."

We crept out of the oak, and I thanked it silently for its brief respite of shelter. The moon shone bright overhead, a good omen, and lit the way to the northern path. I had never been scared in the forest before this night. Patrick reached for my hand.

A presence lurked behind us. I held the acorns, the seeds of strength, murmuring quiet incantations, to stave it off as we pushed through the tangle of hazel shrubs. He followed us. Footsteps. The hazel cleared and the northern path lay ahead. Patrick tightened his grip on my hand, and I knew, despite his prayers, he was as scared as I was.

The cleared path made our journey easier.

"We'll be coming to the meadow soon," I said.

Grateful the light from Cill Dara shone into the forest, Patrick and I ran together, eager to reach the safety of Cill Dara's grounds. I fought to keep up with Patrick's long strides. Then, he halted suddenly.

"Keep going," I urged him. Maithghean was close. Patrick stepped aside, and I saw the reason for our stop.

The man with whom I had shared a lifetime stood before us. Bres. I blinked, unable to process what I saw. Bres's familiar amber eyes glowed, and his long hair was pulled back.

"Brigid." He smiled his same sinister smile of eons ago.

My heart leapt into my throat, and all my confidence drained from me. I backed away.

"Who is he?" Patrick asked, confused. He looked for the old magician, not a handsome hunter, clad in leather.

"Bres." I watched the man I had not seen for lifetimes with unaccountable fascination. Bres walked closer, his wiry muscles evident beneath his leggings. He was wearing the ancient leather dress and even kept his supply of arrows strapped to his back, as I had last seen him, when we buried our son. "How are you here?"

"Brigid, my wife, I've come to take you home with me." He pronounced my name in the old way, *breed, bride*. His eyes glinted toward Patrick as he brought my hand to his lips, just as he had on our wedding day.

"She's not yours to take," Patrick pulled my hand away from Bres's lips. "I remember you..." Patrick said the words so softly, so faintly, that they barely registered with me.

Bres mesmerized me as our eyes held. The earth warmed beneath my feet, a clue a spell surrounded me. I couldn't do anything to stop it. The magic blanketed me, smooth, comforting, and I couldn't have fought it, even if I wanted to. I languished, dazed. Bres, the father of my son. Ruadan, my boy.

"Brigid!" Patrick shook me. "It's a trick. Don't listen to him. Bres has been dead for many years."

"So have I." I reached for my husband's hand. Bres caused me heartache, so much pain, and unhappiness. Yet, from our marriage I bore our son, I learned arts, I sang poems. I drifted back into early memories of that life. Bres was all I had when the Danann abandoned me to the enemy tribe. For a short time, we cared for each other. We had been united against those who betrayed us, until he betrayed me. I remembered his ferocity, his intensity, his arrogance. Cautiously, I lifted my fingers to his hair, remembering the thick silkiness. His touch was familiar, and his heat radiated through me.

"Come with me, Brigid," he said. He looked up at Patrick, grinning at his confusion. "I'm taking Brigid to our son, *Padraic*."

"Our son?" I moved closer, bathed in the heat of his stare. I was aware of the magic, from some distant spot in my mind, but it didn't matter. A mother's love for her child is a cord uncut by time.

"Ruadan awaits his mother's return."

"My son is alive?" I fell deeper into his spell, into the sturdiness of his hand. I wanted to see Ruadan, so lost and unfairly slain. He was back. Bres said he was. He loved his boy as much as I did. Ruadan was the only person who could bring out the goodness in Bres. The love for our child was the tie that held us together through lifetimes.

"Brigid, no!" Patrick's voice, Padraic's voice was remote, a stranger who called from far away.

CHAPTER 39
Patrick and Brigid

Patrick watched in horror as she followed Maithghean or Bres back into the darkness of the forest. Brigid was entranced in a spell created by evil. Patrick saw both men, alternating between Bres and Maithghean, but Brigid only saw Bres. He enticed her with stories of her son, dead for ages.

"I know you," he said as Brigid walked into the forest with Bres or a mirage of Bres. Patrick had seen him before. He knew his face. Things in his mind began to fit into place, like wooden puzzle pieces, like a key into a lock. Brigid's claims always felt familiar, but they were vague, hazy, like a dream. The dreams he'd had were more real than the memories. Now, here they were. He felt the earth sink beneath him and recognized he could do this if he chose.

In Padraic's past, he'd hidden this from his Fomorian mother. Outcast as a child, he possessed the bearing of his unknown Danann father. He had light-colored eyes. He had the ability to blend into anything on the earth. He hated it as a child. It kept him different from the rest. Then he understood, after many misguided attempts, his secret skill was strength. A secret, his mother warned. Don't let the Fomorians know. Practice, practice. He became obsessed with it. He worked with stone, with oak, with the field, with the sea. Then Brigid appeared, the one person who understood his isolation and his abilities. She held Bres's hand for her wedding vows, but his eyes met hers, even as she was married to another. Later, she ran across his fields...

Even before, they'd known each other. More memories fell into place. The battles. Sword to sword against Bres. Padraic spared his life because of this. The man was Ruadan's father. Brigid would always be tied to him. Patrick, Padraic, couldn't be responsible for his death.

Patrick started after them, but realized he couldn't help her alone. He was no longer Padraic, not a warrior, not a Danann. He was a priest. He served God, one who brought light into the world, not a worshiper of sacrifices and spells.

He sprinted back to Cill Dara, terrified to think he wasted precious time.

"Please, help me," he said to the praying nuns and monks in the chapel. They jumped up in surprise, wondering why the missing priest from Armagh suddenly appeared before them.

Brother Ultan approached him cautiously. "Father Patrick, shall I...?"

"Get the chariots. Warn everyone."

Patrick ran back outside into the circle of light. He hesitated, expecting the light to burn, or to be transported to heaven. It was only the light created by the druids. Their intense concentration was evident as the circle grew and surrounded the chapel. Frantically, he ran through the circle looking for Darlughdacha. Mariah went with him. He stopped, winded. He was not a young man anymore.

"Brigid needs help. He's taken her," he said to the druids. Panic rose within him. He knew how to deal with stubborn kings and battle-hardened warriors. He could turn their eyes to God. He didn't know how to deal with this mystical evil, a man who could change from one person to another and disappear into the night.

"They can't break the circle. She told us earlier," Mariah whispered to him. "If Dar leaves now, the light will be gone. Cill Dara will be unprotected."

He dropped to his knees inside the circle of silent druids, illuminated by light. "God have mercy," he said. "Please let me find her. She may not be a Christian in your eyes, but she's a good woman. Please allow no harm to come to her."

They probably headed back to Fotharit. What would her father say when she reappeared? Would no one there question her life as a slave? Would they care?

He wants to harness old powers. Patrick recalled Brigid's words. Maithghean wouldn't waste his time forcing her into slavery. He would use whatever evil he could to harness her...her what? Energy? Her very soul? Patrick trembled at the unholy thought.

"Ultan, where are you? Bring the chariots," he called again impatiently to the confused monks who watched from the church. They'd heard the whispered rumors about his sudden disappearance, then there he was, leading the charge to find their druid abbess.

The druids, grounded into their rituals, took no apparent notice of the din. Like fervent prayer, Patrick understood why they couldn't be disturbed, as white light flooded from their center. He prayed too, that their spells would work. Suddenly, he heard Dar's voice in his head. "Go to her," she said silently. "We will do our work here."

Patrick ran to the chariot. "Aren't you putting yourself in danger? The British men are searching for you," asked Ultan.

"It doesn't matter. She must be found." They pounded north in the chariot, and Patrick strained to see through the darkness for any shape or form. A sudden thought came to him as they splashed across the river. Maithghean wouldn't take the main road. He would hide, conniving in the forest.

"Go into the forest. Follow the trail."

Ultan did as he was told, clutching the reins as the chariot careened across the meadow into the embrace of tall ancient oaks.

They were just here. He recognized the path. He and Brigid had hidden in the hollows of one of these trees. Patrick's thoughts ran riot, a formless wire of incoherent worry. He'd always been able to save her, in dreams and visions. This is reality. He took note of the shuddering branches and the cold wind that blew in from the sea. He recognized the scent of that sea from years spent alone on the hills, yearning for escape.

"Father Patrick, how far should we go?" The shadows loomed. The moon was full, yet its light didn't shine through the trees. Evil is here, Patrick thought. I can feel it. Just like in the visions. He began to dissect the dreams he and Brigid shared. How did I find her then? We were always together. It just happened.

Screams tore through the forest and iced his spine. A woman's scream. A wolf's howl. Motioning to Ultan to stop the horses, he waited for the evil to show itself.

"Patrick."

He stepped out of the chariot and turned toward the voice behind him.

"Brigid?" He reached to her and saw that she was bound to a giant oak.

"I'm sorry, Patrick. I didn't know. He wove a powerful spell..." she said. He touched her face, wet with tears.

"Are you well, Brigid? Has he hurt you?"

"Not yet. He's planning to sacrifice both of us, you and me, to take our ancient powers."

His heart lurched and all of the horrible stories he heard growing up in Britannia rang true. Druids. Human sacrifice. Ultan made a small sound behind him.

"Ultan, go get help," he commanded. "Bring the guards from Dun Ailenn, as many as you can find. Cill Dara isn't in danger. Only Brigid is. Bring holy water from the well and as many monks with weapons that will join you. Travel through the field, where the moon will light your path."

Ultan urged the horses to return the way they came.

"Maithghean has figured out a way to harness the power," said Brigid. "That's how he can change, shape-shift, like the ancients. He became a wolf. He became Bres."

Patrick groped with the cords at Brigid's wrists, remembering a time when his own hands were tied with tight wrist-cutting rope. He wished again, not for the first time in his life, for a knife.

"Brigid, where's your dagger?" Then he remembered: it lay on the floor of the cellar, where he made her drop it.

"I'm sorry, Patrick," she said. "Ruadan isn't here. It was all a trick, and powerful magic. I should have known."

"Shh..." He stroked her hair, a futile gesture given their present situation. "Look toward Cill Dara." A faint luminescence shone. The light gave him hope perhaps the good magic and the grace of God would save them.

He tried to untie the knots around her wrists, and he suddenly knew how Siculus must have felt, a servant dying in order to save an adolescent boy's life. Patrick glanced over his shoulder, praying the wicked man wouldn't slice open his neck from behind.

"Brigid, these knots are in some kind of pattern. I can't get them undone." Patrick untied one but then the one beneath it tightened. Brigid flinched.

"It's a sacrificer's pattern," she said. "I don't know it well. How many knots are there?"

"Seven, including the one I've just undone. They each seem to be triple knot-ted."

"It is a sacred pattern, used only for prisoners in sacrifice, symbolizing their gift of death to the land. Please, Patrick, remove the knots carefully, following my instructions." Patrick listened as she explained how to untie each knot backwards, to undo the spell entwined in the knots. A day ago, he would have laughed at silly notions of spells and knots, but he saw Maithghean and knew now black magic did exist.

A wolf howled again. "It's him. Maithghean," Brigid whispered. "He's shape-shifted into the wolf." She seemed exhausted, her energy sapped from the illusion that had been put upon her. Patrick picked up a stout stick and hid it next to him, behind the tree. He continued to reverse the knotted pattern. Brigid's hands were cold from their tight bindings.

"Your stick will do no good," she said. "His power is strong, not defeated by physical force. I've failed. I failed you, and I failed the ancient ones. I've allowed evil to run rampant in Éire."

"You have not failed. Not yet. Ultan has gone for help and we will be in the meadow soon." Patrick hoped his words reassured her, as his hands trembled with fear.

A razor sharp pain tore at my shoulder, and I thought the tree branches had snared me. Nausea filled my gut as I gasped in agony. It was not a branch but Maithghean's hand, gnarled with long yellow fingernails that ripped at my arm. The scratch looked like those that had covered Conleth's body. He dropped an assorted pile of stones and herbs in front of me and gathered kindling for a fire, elements of magic, similar to the stones and acorns in my skirt pocket, except I would never use the gifts from the earth in the way he did.

Patrick kept a tight grip on my hands on the opposite side of the wide oak. Too engrossed in his sacrificial preparations, Maithghean didn't know Patrick was there. The shredded wound festered on my shoulder, as if I had been mauled by a wolf.

"I will have all of your powers," Maithghean seethed as flames licked the sticks of oak and hazel. "I can capture them. I've become a wolf. I've been an illusion of someone else." Maithghean's face shifted in and out of focus, effects of lingering magic, alternating between handsome Bres and the withered old man.

The ties loosened as Patrick, behind the oak, worked on the last two knots. I prayed he followed the proper order. Maithghean arranged chunks of quartz in a circle around the bonfire, chanting incantations as he worked. I had the barest minimum of training in the sacrificial arts and dimly recalled the spell he wove.

"No." I said the word aloud. Anything I could do to disturb his concentration would gain time for Patrick to undo the knots. Then what? I pushed the pessimistic thought from my mind.

Maithghean glanced at me as he placed the last stone. The firelight glinted through the crystal facets. I knew these stones. Just the right connection between light and quartz would create more flames. With the oak and hazel thrown into the quartzite flames, he'd have powerful energy. The crystals themselves were not dangerous. The danger came from Maithghean's evil intentions, the darkness he would shift into the energy formed by the elements. He began to chant, whispering dark, ancient words. Not only did he want to take me, but the soul of the forest, the spirit of earth, of Danu, too.

The last knot snapped free and my arms swung forward. I tried to flex my hands but they hung like dead weight at my side, numb and useless. Patrick stepped out from behind the oak and picked up a branch. He strode forward

and slammed it against the back of Maithghean's skull. Then Patrick held the branch above him, ready to gouge it into Maithghean's heart.

"Don't" I said. "You can't kill. You mustn't."

The point of his staff touched Maithghean's shrunken chest, and the old man watched Patrick and me, engaged in our own battle of wills.

I've killed once for you, Patrick told me silently. An image of Conleth on the battlefield, smashing the warrior's skull with the oak staff flashed between us. He would do it again.

"No," I said. "He will not die. He will always be able to return in some form or another. We must help him leave this earth, but not through murder." Maithghean, although withered and old, still had a glint in his yellow eye. Slowly, he unfolded himself from his crumpled spot on the ground.

I reached for the strength of the spirits beneath me. Please, I hurled one last thought to the Túatha de Danann below with every part of my being. It was not fair, I knew, to ask again for the Túatha de Danann to sustain me and Patrick. *Please,* I begged. *Find for him the power of who he once was.*

A rush of energy overwhelmed us, and the presence of Lugh, Nuada, Eiru, Macha, and Dagda—all of the Danann—united with us. They gathered their energies, stored within the earth. This final fight would be their last. *You can't save us. Patrick can't save us. Only we can save ourselves.*

Thank you, I said to them. The burden of guilt I carried my entire life evaporated with their acknowledgement. Energy soared into me as never before. The goddess light rose up from the ground, and power gained from all my previous lives filled me. I rose over the old magician. I saw his sickness, his desperate need to gain what was not his, out of jealousy and greed. His soul was murky, overcome with a dripping blackness that could never come clean. The figure at our feet convulsed.

I held myself over him, supported by Túatha de Danann. Patrick took my hand. The spark of fire between us, the tie that bound us from one lifetime to the next, grew. Our hands clasped, were no longer two separate entities, but an extension of each other. Light flowed through us, around us. I recited ancient spells, and he said prayers to God. Though the words were different, it didn't matter. Christian and druid linked their purpose together: a basic need for good to defeat evil.

Our white light, calm and soothing, enveloped Maithghean, who he bucked against it, a refusal of its peace. The magician's resistance continued as he slowly weakened. Dawn edged a thin line on the horizon, its pink and gold rays rose. A single beam reached ahead and touched the man worn by lifetimes of hate. Quietly, Maithghean dissipated, as mist does when touched by the sun.

Then, all was still. Patrick and I collapsed next to the circle of quartz and watched light embrace the sky.

Bibliography

Barry, Terry. *History of Settlement in Ireland*. London: Routledge, 1999.

Bitel, Lisa M. St. "Brigit of Ireland: From Virgin Saint to Fertility Goddess." Monastic Matrix. February 2001. http://monasticmatrix.osu.edu/comm entaria/st-brigit-ireland.

Bury, J.B. The Life of St. Patrick and His Place in History. London: Macmillian, 1905 (reprinted).

Cahill, Thomas. *How the Irish Saved Civilization*. New York: Doubleday, 1995.

Charles-Edwards, T.M. *Early Christian Ireland*. Cambridge: Cambridge University Press, 2000.

Condren, Mary. *The Serpent and the Goddess: Women, Religion and Power in Celtic Ireland*. New York: Harper Collins, 1989.

de Paor, Liam. *Saint Patrick's World*. Notre Dame: University of Notre Dame Press, 1993.

de Paor, Maire. Patrick: *The Pilgrim Apostle of Ireland*. New York: Harper Collins, 1998.

Ellis, Peter B. *Celtic Women: Women in Celtic Society and Literature*. Grand Rapids: William B. Eerdmans Publishing Company, 1995.

Ellis, Peter B. *Druids*. Grand Rapids: William B. Eerdmans Publishing Company, 1994.

Flanagan, Laurence, (Compiled by). *Irish Women's Letters*. New York: St. Martin's Press, 1997.

Freeman, Philip. *St. Patrick of Ireland*. New York: Simon and Schuster, 2004.

Freeman, Philip. *War, Women and Druids*. Austin: University of Texas Press, 2002.

Gallico, Paul. *The Steadfast Man: A Life of St. Patrick*. London: Michael Joseph, 1958.

Greenhill, Basil. *The Archaeology of Boats and Ships*. London: Conway Maritime Press, 1995.

Gregory, Lady Isabella Augusta. *Irish Myths and Legends*. London: Running Press, 1998. (reprinted from 1910, John Murray, publisher)

Matthews, Caitlin, and John. *Encyclopedia of Celtic Wisdom*. Shaftesbury: Element Books Ltd, 1994.

McDonald, Theresa. *Achill Island: Archaeology, History and Folklore*. Tullamore: I.A.S. Publications, 1997.

McColman, Carl. "Is Brigid a Pagan Goddess or a Christian Saint? Yes." Retrieved from: www.beliefnet.com 7/29/2005, First published in Atlanta Celtic Quarterly.

MacCana Proinsias. *Celtic Mythology: Library of the World's Myths and Legends*. New York: Peter Bedrick Books, 1985.

MacManus, Seamus. *The Story of the Irish Race*. New York: Random House, 1921 original – 1990 revised edition.

McCone, Kim. "Brigit in the Seventh Century: A Saint With Three Lives?" *Peritia* 1 (1982), 107-145.

Ó Cróinín, Dáibhí. *Early Medieval Ireland*. London: Longman. 1995.

Ranelagh, John O'Beirne. *A Short History of Ireland*. Cambridge: Cambridge University Press, 1994.

Simmons, Paula and Ekarius, Carol. *Storey's Guide to Raising Sheep*. Pownal: Storey Books, 2000.

Squire, Charles. *Celtic Myths and Legends*. Bath: Parragon, 2003.

Starhawk. *The Spiral Dance: A Rebirth of the Ancient Religion of the Great Goddess*. San Francisco: Harper and Row, 1989.

Stokes, Whitley (trans) and Murphy, Ruth (compiled). "On the Life of St. Brigit." www.ucc.ie/celt: Corpus of Electronic Texts, CELT online at University College, Cork, Ireland. Text ID Number: T201010.

About Author

Sheila R. Lamb's short stories are published in a variety of literary journals and she's been a writer-in-residence at Weymouth Center for the Arts and Humanities, a fellow at the Virginia Center for the Creative Arts (VCCA), and a contributor at Sewanee Writers' Conference. She has a long-standing fascination with Irish history and participated in Achill Island Archaeology Field School in County Mayo. During the day, she teaches history in the mountains of Virginia. She is the author of *Once a Goddess* and *Fiery Arrow*. *Church of the Oak* is the final book in the Brigid of Ireland trilogy. Follow Sheila on social media @sheilarlamb and on her website at sheilarlamb.com.

Photo © Shannon Hibberd

www.ingramcontent.com/pod-product-compliance
Lightning Source LLC
Chambersburg PA
CBHW020009140726
47904CB00018B/2133